SILENCE CAN BE DEADLY

Trouble in Pleasant Valley • Book Three

Deborah Sprinkle

Published by Scrivenings Press LLC
15 Lucky Lane
Morrilton, Arkansas 72110
https://ScriveningsPress.com

Printed in the United States of America

Hardcover ISBN 978-1-64917-159-7
Paperback ISBN 978-1-64917-158-0
eBook ISBN 978-1-64917-160-3

Library of Congress Control Number: 2021948007

Editors: DiAnn Mills and Linda Fulkerson

Cover by Linda Fulkerson, www.bookmarketinggraphics.com

All characters are fictional, and any resemblance to real people, either factual or historical, is purely coincidental.

Scripture quotations are taken from the Holy Bible, New Living Translation, copyright ©1996, 2004, 2015 by Tyndale House Foundation. Used by permission of Tyndale House Publishers, Carol Stream, Illinois 60188. All rights reserved.

An entertaining read, full of pulse-pounding tension. A great mix of suspense and romance. Don't miss *Silence Can be Deadly*.

— Darlene L. Turner, bestselling and award-winning author

Prepare yourself for a wild ride! *Silence can be Deadly* will spin you into orbit.

— DiAnn Mills, Christy Award Winner and former director of the Blue Ridge Mountains Christian Writers Conference

Deborah Sprinkle has done it again with *Silence Can Be Deadly*. This page-turner will have you on the edge of your seat until "The End."

— Patricia Bradley author of the Logan Point Series, Memphis Cold Case Novels, and the Natchez Trace Park Ranger Series

To all the beautiful souls who support, encourage, and pray me through each book. I couldn't do it without you!

ACKNOWLEDGMENTS

How many times have you heard the phrase "it takes a village?" In my writing, as in so many other aspects of my life, I've found this to be true. Google is great, but it only gets me so far, and then I find myself in need of the wisdom and experience that can only come from people who have lived through an experience or worked a job.

People like CW3 Larry Myers, US Army (Ret) who helped me put together Peter's backstory in Afghanistan. His experience in the Army CID proved invaluable. I'm blessed to call him and his wonderful wife, Nancy, friends.

Then there's Deputy Samuel Crews of the Memphis Police Department. A crazy circumstance—that I won't get into here—brought us together and he graciously agreed to help me with any questions I might have about police procedure. Deputy Crews helped me with questions I had related to my book. Among other questions, some about the relationship between police and private investigators.

My village is growing, and all I can say is—I can use all the help I can get!

On the craft side of things, there is my constant friend, DiAnn Mills, who once again helped me with her editing skills to make my book as good as it can be. Thank you from the bottom of my heart.

To the owner of Scrivenings Press, Linda Fulkerson, thank you again for believing in my writing, for your encouragement, and for sharing your talents and wisdom.

And then there's my posse. Sandra M. Hart, Bonnie Beardsley, Starr Ayers, K. Denise Holmberg, and Linda Dindzans. Great writers all who keep me on my toes. Iron sharpens iron and this group proves it. I love writing and doing life with them.

Above all else, I thank God who determines our steps and brought my village together—especially me and my husband, Les, my biggest fan, the love of my life.

And all the people said Amen!

1

Peter Grace angled his taxicab into the curb as skillfully as he once traversed the streets of Kabul. His cell phone lit up and skittered across the seat next to him. A number appeared he hadn't seen in three years, and his hands curled around the steering wheel, the muscles in his arms straining against his T-shirt. His last conversation with Lawrence Merton brought him nothing but misery.

He stared at the text box.

In town. Need to see you. Urgent. Call me. L

Memories from Afghanistan flooded his brain, threatening to wreck his hard-won peace. No way. His life may not be the greatest, but it was his, and he wanted to keep it. Lawrence was not going to get another chance to turn his world upside down.

"Peter, are you all right?" a soft voice said from the back seat.

He blinked. "Yes, Mrs. G. I'm fine." He jogged around the taxi and helped the frail woman onto the sidewalk.

"What do I owe you?" She opened her small purse.

Peter laid a hand on her slim fingers. "We'll settle up later. Okay?"

She raised blue eyes, cloudy with cataracts. "If you don't mind. I can't seem to find my wallet."

"Not a problem."

She patted his arm. "You're a kind soul, Peter. Be sure to tell your grandmother hello for me."

"I will. Now go inside. I'll see you next week." Peter returned to his taxi and checked his mirrors. He caught sight of Mrs. G as her front door closed behind her. This was his life now—driving taxi and helping people when he could. Nobody was going to mess it up for him.

Especially Lawrence Merton.

"Fifty-two. Come in." Peter's radio squawked.

"Go ahead."

"Got time for one more?"

He looked at the time. "Where?"

"The airport."

PETER PICKED the man up at Lambert airport and, after a brief exchange, headed for downtown St. Louis. Ex-military, judging by the man's physique and haircut. Flat dark eyes. Streetlights glinted off a large gold watch. Right wrist. Heavy gold ring. Left ring finger.

Details. A habit honed in Army Intelligence.

They rode in silence through Friday night traffic on Highway 70. He lowered his visor and glanced at the photograph of a cabin in the woods clipped to the underside. Someday, when he had enough money saved.

"What is that?" the man said.

"Nothing important." Peter flipped the picture out of sight.

"It must be important to you. You keep it where other men keep pictures of their children."

Peter eyed the shadowed face in the rearview mirror. A hint of an accent. "It's a place I used to go."

"And?"

And none of your business. "I'd like to go back. That's all."

Peter divided his time between glancing in the mirror and watching the traffic. Something about the man and his questions made the hairs on the back of his neck stand up.

The man's cell phone rang. He pulled it from his coat pocket and spoke in low tones.

The sooner he got this guy to his hotel, the better.

His controlled movements and expressionless face set off alarm bells. He'd seen guys like him before in—

Screeching tires jerked Peter's attention forward. Red lights blazed. Horns blared. Cars on both sides. No escape. He stomped the brakes and braced for impact. "Hang on back there."

No bang of colliding cars, but Peter cringed as his passenger hit the Plexiglas shield between the front and back seats. Judging by the colorful language, Peter could kiss a tip goodbye.

Peter swiveled in his seat. "Sorry. You okay?"

"Nothing a good plastic surgeon cannot fix."

Slavic?

The man gathered papers from the floor and placed them in his open briefcase. "What happened?"

Peter's skin prickled. No anger from the man. Tight control.

"Who knows? Friday night in the big city." Peter returned his attention to the road.

After a few miles, he flipped on his right turn signal. "First time in St. Louis?"

"Yes."

"There's a lot to do here. If you get a chance." He merged into traffic on Broadway. Almost there.

"Maybe next time." The man clipped his words.

Possibly Russian?

Peter turned right onto Pine Street. Four blocks later, he pulled into the circle drive of the Omni Hotel. The muscles in his jaw relaxed.

"Here you go." Peter hurried to open the passenger's door. "Again, I apologize for the sudden stop."

"No problem." The man stepped out.

Agile. Athletic.

The hotel doorman appeared from nowhere and reached for the briefcase, but the man tucked it under his arm. "I will take this one."

"Of course. I'll just check to be sure you haven't forgotten anything." He ducked inside the open taxi door.

Peter retrieved his fare's suitcase from the trunk.

The passenger moved to the rear of the taxi He glanced at the uniformed man waiting on the curb. "Are hotel personnel usually this eager in St. Louis?"

"Must be new." Peter shrugged. "Never seen him before."

"If my calculations are correct, this should be enough—plus a little extra." The man handed Peter a thick wad of folded bills.

"Thank you."

"Do you have a card?"

"In case you need to see a plastic surgeon?" A joke that could become a nightmare.

"Right." The man grinned

Peter pulled one from a small stack held together with a rubber band.

"I will need a ride to the airport tomorrow after my business is concluded."

His teeth gleamed in the bright lights of the entrance to the hotel, but his eyes remained devoid of warmth. Like a snake.

Peter handed the suitcase off to the doorman and slammed the trunk lid. He watched his passenger cross the hotel lobby. The man moved like he owned the place.

Peter kneaded the back of his neck. Something told him he would see this man again.

But not to give him a ride.

2

─────────

The car wash vacuum emitted a high-pitched whine. Peter gritted his teeth and pulled the hose from under the seat. He yanked the manila envelope off the intake, and the vacuum's sound settled back to a dull roar. He scanned the front and back before sliding it through the opened shield onto the front seat. Nothing written on the outside of the envelope. He'd finish cleaning his taxi and decide what to do next.

Tired after a long day of hauling people from point A to point B, he rubbed his eyes with the palms of his hands and dropped onto the driver's seat. His gaze drifted to the parcel lying next to him. Had to belong to his last fare. Must have slid from the passenger's briefcase when it fell on the floor. All his other passengers today had been families, older couples, or people he knew. He should deliver it to the hotel. The guy said he was only there for tonight. Probably something he needed tomorrow. But what would Peter say once he got there? Mr. Snake Eyes paid in cash.

"Hi. I need to get this to a businessman who's staying here. You know, the one who came in wearing a gray suit and carrying a briefcase."

Right. Not too many of those staying at the Omni tonight.

He shook his head. The place would be full of men fitting that description.

Peter gazed out the window at the full moon. He glanced at the envelope once more. Maybe he should check inside. It might have the guy's name on it. Or it could be empty.

One sheet of paper. No name. A detailed itinerary for tomorrow. If it was his passenger's, he planned to eat every meal on the Hill. He must really like the famed Italian section of St. Louis. And he had a press conference scheduled mid-morning.

Peter scanned the itinerary again.

*Breakfast

But Snake Eyes didn't seem the type to be holding a press conference. Involved with the trip? His gut told him this guy wasn't part of an entourage either—not even security. The silk suit. His watch and ring. All wrong.

Who could the itinerary belong to? Nothing in the news about a visit from someone important. And why would Snake Eyes have this info in his briefcase?

Peter tapped the steering wheel with his fist. Something bad was going down. And once more, he'd been dropped on the front line.

Last time he uncovered something illegal, the crooks threatened his grandparents. Forced him to keep silent, and his life imploded. The same vibe pulsed through him now.

One thing for sure, Peter wasn't going anywhere near the Omni Hotel or the Hill if he went out at all. He shook his head. He'd stay in his little south side neighborhood. No more mister upstanding citizen. He'd tried in the Army and look where that got him.

Banished from a career he loved and driving a cab.

He wrenched the key in the ignition. The cab roared to life and the delicate cross hanging from his mirror swayed. Light filtering through his windshield caught the motion. Peter reached to steady it. Mom's. The only thing he had left. *God, he missed her*. She'd tell him to stop wasting time feeling sorry for himself and get on with life. Peter drew in a deep breath and let it out. And she'd be right—as always. He drove to his apartment and parked his taxi in the back like usual.

He brushed the photo of the cabin with his fingertips. One day he'd go back. Those were his happiest times, as close to a real home as he'd ever known. He flipped the visor up with a decisive thud.

One leg out of the cab, he stopped. He yanked the visor down and grabbed the picture. Reaching across the dashboard, he removed the necklace and pooled the fine silver chain in his palm. He slammed the door, beeped it locked, and walked away—the worrisome document clutched in his hand.

Inside his apartment, he lay the envelope next to the kitchen sink and retrieved a box of matches. He'd destroy the whole thing and forget he ever saw it. The match flared and fire climbed the slim wooden stick. Pain from the searing heat hit his fingertips before he dropped the match into the sink and ran water on it. Staring at the black mark left on the stainless steel, he knew he couldn't set fire to evidence. Too many years of gathering intel.

One. Two. Three boards from the refrigerator. He slipped a screwdriver under the edge, working it carefully along the seam. The piece of flooring came loose with a soft pop. He opened his hidey-hole, folded the paper into the tight space, and toed the rug back in place.

His body and mind craved sleep. He would think about it tomorrow after he'd rested.

3

———

Peter valued information of all kinds. Another by-product of his days in the Army. His fellow taxi drivers called him a news junky. They were probably right. He tuned his TV to FOX News before getting out of bed in the morning, and he often fell asleep to CNN. His phone gave him hourly headline updates.

The morning after his meeting with Snake Eyes, Peter slept in. He woke at nine and clicked the remote.

"Breaking News: Former defense contractor Lawrence Merton has been shot."

He heaved himself upright, his thumb pressing hard on the volume button. A sour taste filled his mouth.

"It was a grisly scene at a local restaurant in St. Louis this morning as Lawrence Merton was gunned down while eating breakfast before delivering a press conference. A sniper's bullet punched through the window and into his skull. He was pronounced dead at Barnes-Jewish Hospital. Mr. Merton lost his invalid wife Ethel three months ago. It is unsure why Mr. Merton was holding the press conference, but some speculate he was about to uncover ongoing government fraud.

Peter swung his legs out of bed. That's what Lawrence wanted when he texted last night. *God forgive me.* What a fool

9

he'd been. If only he'd called him back. Peter sat on the edge of his bed, his elbows on his knees. He buried his face in his hands.

Maybe if he'd returned the text, Lawrence would be alive today. He raised his head and stared at the wall in front of him.

Or Lawrence would still be dead, and he'd be in the middle of an investigation—one that threatened to break his life wide open and endanger those he loved. His mind swirled with images from the past and yesterday. He couldn't think. Maybe food would help.

He switched on the coffeepot and placed wholegrain bread in the toaster. In the living area, he switched to another news channel for their take. The aromas of coffee and toast soon filled the apartment. He chewed absently and paced back and forth.

At the window, he stared in the direction of his cab. The schedule. The asterisk by breakfast. His stomach churned. The itinerary belonged to Lawrence.

Snake Eyes killed Lawrence Merton. The so-called business he had in town.

Why did Peter have to open the stupid envelope? Why hadn't he thrown it in the trash at the car wash? Peter's gaze unfocused as he recalled every detail of the man's face. He'd seen faces like his before.

Men without hearts. Men without souls. Men who killed without remorse.

So what now? If he went to the police, they'd soon figure out he knew Lawrence and find their past connection. He couldn't let that happen. A roar of frustration threatened to erupt from his throat. How could he do nothing knowing who murdered his former friend, a man who reached out to him in the last moments of his life?

But Peter had his grandmother to protect.

And there was something else. He stopped chewing. The assassin couldn't afford to leave Peter breathing.

Not when he realized where he'd lost the file. Too risky.

Once again Peter was forced to leave his life and go to ground. He tossed the remainder of his toast in the trash.

His phone rang.

A number from the Omni Hotel.

Once. Twice. Three rings.

Silence.

Stay cool. He massaged his fist with his left hand. Remember what he was taught. Think. Plan. Execute.

He must vanish. Turning, he kicked the throw rug to one side. In the space below, the manila envelope lay atop two clear bags filled with money and papers.

He made three copies of Merton's schedule. One he prepared to mail to himself at a post office box. The original he folded and stuck in his wallet.

The other two copies went to the two men in this world who Peter trusted with his life. One outside Washington, D.C., and the other in Pleasant Valley, Ohio. Each with a letter of direction.

To be opened upon notification of my death.

Peter lifted a blue rag from the bottom of the hole. The bundle contained a Beretta M9. Been a long time since he'd shot a weapon. He'd need some practice. Tonight, he'd head to the gun range.

But first, he needed to convince Grandma Kate to leave town.

4

———————

Clouds gathered in the west as Peter parked in front of Grandma Kate's south St. Louis home. A sturdy brick bungalow and a perfect carpet of green grass rivaled the neighborhood. How she managed by herself after his grandfather's death never ceased to amaze him. He'd offered to help numerous times, but she refused. She needed to keep busy —at least that was what she told him. A gust of wind caught the flag hanging from a post of the covered porch.

Peter trudged up the sidewalk and mounted the stairs to his grandmother's door. He'd decided to tell her everything—about Afghanistan, Lawrence, the assassin, the whole thing. Maybe then she'd agree to go away, and he could concentrate knowing she was safe.

The door opened before he could ring the bell.

"Peter. What a lovely surprise." The older woman unlocked the storm door and held it wide for him to enter. With both doors closed and fastened, she turned and opened her arms. "My favorite grandson."

He chuckled. "Your only grandson, Grandma."

She wagged a finger at him with a grin. "But still my

13

favorite." She led him down a short hall to a small kitchen in the back. "Sit. Something to drink?"

"Got any root beer?"

"Of course. I keep some special for you." She popped the caps on two bottles and sat across from him. "What's the matter, my boy?"

Peter ran his finger down the dark brown bottle. He wasn't sure where to begin. How would his grandmother feel about him when she learned what he'd done? Her opinion of him meant more to him than anyone else's on earth.

She reached for his hand. "Grandson, whatever it is, I will always be here for you. I will always love you."

Peter gazed at the hand covering his—tanned from working outdoors, spotted and wrinkled with age—the hand of the woman who took care of him when his mother could not. He could not lose her. "I need to tell you something important, Grandma, and I need you to pay attention."

"When I was in Afghanistan, I discovered fraud involving the transport company, and an old friend of mine, Lawrence Merton." He stopped pacing.

"Isn't he—" Her eyes widened.

Peter nodded.

"I messed up, Grandma." He sunk into the chair across from her. "They threatened to kill you and Grandpa, and they planted money in my account to make it seem as if I was involved. I ... let it go, left the Army, and used the money to buy my cab. I haven't had any contact with Merton since then. Until yesterday."

"Lawrence texted me for help. But I ignored him." Peter stood. "I think he was going to come clean, at least I want to believe so. And the worst part is I have proof who did it." He ran a hand through his short hair. "But if I go to the police, everything will come out. They might even think I had something to do with his death." He studied his grandmother's face for an initial reaction.

Was she disappointed in him? Hurt? Sad? Anxiety curdled his stomach. He'd been in combat, but never felt like this before. He couldn't stand it any longer. "Please, say something."

"I wish you had come to me sooner." She gave him a sweet smile. "I had no idea you were struggling with all this on your own."

"You're not disappointed in me?" Relief flooded his system as if he were a child.

"Why would I be? You were protecting the people you love." She lifted her chin. "But now I know what's going on. We need a plan of action."

"That's why I came." He knelt beside her. "Don't you see? The assassin knows who I am too. And by now, he knows I can prove he killed Merton. He can't let me live."

He pushed to his feet. "I want you to go to your sister's in Bonne Terre. I need to know your safe."

"You can want what you want, but I'm staying right here." Grandma Kate crossed her arms. "I'll be careful."

"I'm leaving tomorrow."

"I think you're wise."

"I won't be here to protect you." How could he convince her to leave?

"I understand." She slowly made it to her feet and threw their empty root beer bottles in the trash.

"Grandma, please. Be sensible." He placed his hands on her arms. "I don't want to lose you."

"Dear boy." She hugged him. "Trust me. I'll be fine." She moved away and picked up her pad of paper and a pencil. "But to be on the safe side, why don't you take this number. It's my pastor. If you can't get me, call him. He'll know what to do."

"You are unbelievable." Peter stared at her.

"I'll take that as a compliment."

"But you cannot stay here." He reached across the table to capture her hands. "If you stay here, I can't leave. And if I can't leave …"

She locked eyes with him, a slight frown disrupting her normally smooth forehead. "I'll call my sister this evening."

"Thank you." He was trying to keep her safe. So why did he feel like a jerk? "I promise—"

"Don't make promises you can't keep." She rose from her chair with a sigh. "I'll pack my things."

PETER DROVE BACK to his apartment and parked his cab for the last time. He wouldn't be needing it anymore. Time to reinvent himself again. But where? And as what?

He studied the outside of his building. No signs of an intruder. The twigs still balanced precariously on the third step of the fire escape and against his windowsill.

At his door in the hallway, the string he'd placed between the door and its frame when leaving was still in intact. A flicker of hope lit the darkness. But he blew it out before it could take hold. Mr. Snake Eyes wouldn't leave any loose ends. Including Peter.

He had one more thing to do. He cleaned his gun and headed out. The squat nondescript building sat two blocks from his apartment. A simple sign announced Southside Gun Range and Grill. After shooting a few dozen rounds, Peter was satisfied he hadn't lost his skill.

He entered the grill and sat on a stool at the counter.

"The usual?" The waitress grinned.

He nodded. The Southside Grill was his watering hole. He talked guns and hunting with the guys. Shot some pool. The Grill didn't serve alcohol. Which was why he frequented it. He'd been pretty messed up when he first came home from the Army.

But no more. No liquor for over two years. He'd put the past behind him, and in the Grill, he was able to enjoy the camaraderie without the urge to drink.

Until Lawrence Merton's reemergence into his life. *God rest his soul.* As he downed his soft drink, his gaze searched the dim interior for anyone who appeared out of place. No one stood out. But better safe ... He paid for his root beer and smiled at the girl behind the counter. "Mind if I slip out the side tonight?"

"Did ya borrow money from the wrong people, Peter?" She snorted as she swept a rag across the smooth surface. "Or is there some husband after your hide?"

"Nothing so interesting." He laughed. "It's raining. Shorter way home."

"Go on then." She nodded toward the side door.

The rain had stopped but every shadow hid the silhouette of a man with a gun aimed at his chest. By the time he made it to his building, Peter realized his nerves weren't what they used to be.

He frowned as he approached his door on the second floor landing. The juvenile delinquent in apartment six thought it was cool to swap numbers with him. The kid reasoned that if the police came looking for him, they'd go to the wrong door, and it would give him time to get away.

Now Peter's door had six and the delinquent's had nine. He'd change it back before he left. Right now, he was too tired. Sleep for an hour and then leave. Except he didn't think he'd be able to sleep. He'd stretch out, close his eyes, and try.

He must have dozed off because a sound woke him. *Pop-pop-pop.* Only one thing made that noise. A gun with a suppressor. A cold sweat dampened his shirt. He slid out of bed and moved silently to the door. The apartment was dark except for ambient light filtering through his curtains.

Where had the shots come from?

Floorboards creaked on the landing outside his front door.

Sounded like more than one person.

He held his breath.

The tread on the steps going down to the first floor landing groaned. A change in air pressure as the building's front door opened and closed.

They were gone.

He eased the locks open on his door and waited. Nothing. He slowly cracked the door and surveyed the landing. Empty. Hang on. The door to the punk's apartment stood ajar. Peter padded inside. The young man lay sprawled in his bed. Two shots to the heart and one to the head. Professionals. He didn't touch anything, but as he walked out, his hand hovered over the number nine on the door. If only he'd changed the numbers back earlier. Poor kid would be alive.

An execution meant for Peter. He had the file. He could identify the assassin.

Time to disappear.

But could he?

<h1 style="text-align:center">5</h1>

Peter knew how to start over. He'd done it before, and he could do it again. However, this time *was* different. Before, he did it to protect his family. This time the stakes were higher.

When Peter joined the Army, he intended for it to be his career. Because he had a rare eidetic memory—commonly called a photographic memory—he'd been selected for intelligence. He loved his job and serving his country.

When he'd been forced to leave the Army, he decided to live a simple life. He moved back to St. Louis and bought a taxi. He found an apartment in south St. Louis, one of those old U-shaped complexes back off the street in an area called Dutchtown South. Small, but clean. Uncluttered. Simple.

He went to work every day. Watched a little television. Spent time with his grandparents. Went to bed. Occasionally, on his days off, he hung out at the Grill down the street. Shot some pool and talked with the guys. Simple.

And when he had enough money saved, he intended to find a place on a lake like the one he visited with his grandparents. He'd fish and hunt for his food. There'd be a modest sized close-knit community nearby with a small church. Simple.

But his simple life had been blown apart by a traffic jam. If he hadn't had to stop short, throwing Mr. Snake Eyes briefcase on the floor, his neighbor would be alive, and he'd be going about his business.

Except for one thing. Mr. Snake Eyes murdered Lawrence Merton.

He couldn't get involved with the assassination. Okay. He would start his simple life somewhere else under another name.

But now a young man had been killed because of him. Could he reason that one away too? His fingers touched the delicate cross laying on his kitchen table. He didn't think so. Once the assassin realized his mistake, he wasn't going to stop searching for him, and who knows how many other innocent people might get in the way? He still needed to disappear, but not for good. He'd use the time to plan his next move.

He packed his meager belongings in a duffel bag and once more opened his door to the hallway. First shrugging into an olive-green jacket and cap, he then stuck the gun into his waistband at the small of his back.

When he reached the bottom of the stairs, Peter stopped. Would they be watching the front? Maybe he should use the alley door.

But his cab was parked out back. If they were still around, they'd have eyes on it for sure. The front door might seem less suspicious. Like he was just some guy leaving early for work.

He wished he smoked. He could light up as he left, giving him time to survey the scene. Maybe pretend? Peter grabbed a smashed cigarette from the ashtray by the door. He straightened it as best he could. When he stepped outside, he put it in his mouth and acted like he had a lighter. He moved his eyes over the tops of his cupped hands.

No one. Nothing suspicious.

Time to go.

He bent his head, one hand holding the cigarette and the

other stuffed in his pocket and forced himself into a slow pace. The concrete path from the front door to the sidewalk was two hundred feet—or two Lord's Prayers—long.

6

Viktor Liska leaned on the balcony rail of a luxury hotel in Chicago. He pulled his phone from his pocket. "This better be good news."

"There's been a problem," a voice said.

"Do not tell me about problems. You assured me your men could handle this matter." Viktor's knuckles whitened where he grasped his phone.

"It seems some local thug had switched the room numbers—"

"And those idiots rousted the wrong man?" He unclenched his teeth. He'd had new caps put on last month after getting slammed with a lead pipe. He needed to take better care of his mouth.

"Worse. The guy woke up and pulled a gun—"

"Do not tell me they killed him." He paced across the balcony. "I specifically said no violence."

"I'll take care of it. I've got a couple of guys headed back right now to find the cabby."

"He will be gone by now. You know what to look for. Tear the apartment apart. The cab too." He paused. "Get back to me."

"Yes, sir."

Viktor replaced his phone. He'd left St. Louis right after Lawrence Merton's assassination. Viktor had tried to call the taxi driver, but when he didn't get an answer, he couldn't risk looking for the man himself. So he'd relied on local talent. Always a mistake.

A cabby. How hard could it be? But something was definitely not right.

First, the car he hired to pick him up in St. Louis was canceled without his knowledge. Then, out of all the taxi drivers in St. Louis the one to pick up Viktor at the airport was ex-military intelligence and a former friend of the mark.

He needed to speak with this Peter Grace. Was he a pawn in Peter's game? Or were they both pawns in a game neither knew anything about?

He lifted his wineglass, swirled it, and took a sip. His fingers tightened and with a low growl, he hurled it across the balcony where it shattered against a chaise lounge. He disliked being played.

A dark red stain spread slowly over the pillow. In this light, it resembled blood.

7

———

Peter hated to leave his cab, but once the assassin and his guys figured out their mistake, they'd be all over it—like ants on sugar. One of Grandma's sayings. She was ...

No time for sentiment. He turned into an alley and glanced around. He didn't remember the garage door being so loud. Of course, he never opened it at three in the morning either. The gray, late model Ford F-150 took up most of the space, and it was all Peter could do to squeeze in on the driver's side. The truck had belonged to his grandfather. He passed away last March, but his grandmother kept the insurance and license current. Peter rented the garage under a fictitious name, and since he paid on time, the owner didn't ask any questions.

He backed out slowly, got out, retrieved his duffel from the bed of the truck, and padlocked the garage. Took another moment to scan the area before rolling down the alley. Tires popped on broken glass, twigs, and other trash dropped by garbage trucks.

Now what? Where should he go?

He'd always wanted to visit Kentucky. He paused. Eyes closed. He recalled a United States road map. Navigating the familiar streets of south St. Louis, Peter soon approached the ramp for the U.S. 64 bridge. Lights reflected off the Gateway Arch to his left as he crossed the Mississippi River. A lump formed in his throat. Would he ever see his hometown again?

8

One month had passed since Peter pulled up the gravel driveway in middle Kentucky. The sad little ranch house sitting on ten acres of woods and rock needed lots of work, which was perfect as far as Peter was concerned.

He'd stared out the kitchen window every night for two weeks when it finally occurred to him the three stately trees in the front yard reminded him of something. He dubbed them Father, Son, and Holy Ghost. The Father was to his right, the Son in the middle, and the Holy Ghost to his left. Immediately he'd felt more secure somehow. Maybe he had a chance for a future after all. Maybe even the cabin on the lake ...

Peter dashed inside glad to beat the rain. A late afternoon storm. The big oaks swayed in the wind. Even the Father seemed to be conducting a wild symphony. Black clouds covered the sky, and the world outside grew dark. He reached for the light switch. But before his fingers touched the outlet, a brilliant flash of lightening lit up the yard.

And there he was. The dark silhouette from the nightmares that woke Peter sweating in the belly of the night. Standing next to the largest oak.

He'd been a fool. Trees couldn't protect him from the devil.

Over the booming sound of thunder rolling across the valley, the tinkle of breaking glass sounded, and the sting of a hundred bees burned into his face. Searing pain stabbed his right ear. The stickiness on his fingers was all too familiar. A bullet grazed his earlobe.

He ducked and ran to his bedroom. He yanked the curtains to one side and slid open the window that wasn't a window any longer.

When he'd first moved in, he'd re-sided the house with a slight change. He covered the window on this side and engineered a section he could remove from within. Outside, it seemed as if there were no windows on either side of the house, but inside the window frame was still there. All he had to do was push out the piece of siding from inside and crawl out.

The next part proved tricky. His assassin had not come alone. Others would be covering his back door. But if his reasoning worked, they shouldn't be guarding the sides of the house because it looked as if there were no means of egress. He should be okay, but he'd still need to stay alert.

Slowly he pushed the siding out. A gust of air seized the panel from his hands, carrying it a few feet before dumping it into a pile of leaves. He climbed out and paused. The rain and wind made it impossible to hear anything. But if he couldn't hear them, they couldn't hear him. He hurried into the trees and scanned the scene behind him. No movement. *Breathe.* He was safe.

He shook his head. Not true. Like it or not, once again he possessed knowledge of a crime. Only this time, it wasn't fraud— it was murder.

The first stime, he was coerced into looking the other way. He lost his career in the Army, but there wasn't a threat to his life.

This time, there was no question of ignoring it. This time, it clearly wasn't up to him. Along with the question of whether he lived or died. If he did nothing, the assassin would find him, and he would die.

Time to fight back.

He'd parked his truck in back of a vacant, neighboring house. The bungalow was a seasonal rental, and he'd told the agent he would keep an eye on it. Retrieving his car key from a metal box under a fender, he started his Ford pickup and slowly made his way around the house, relying only on his eyesight to navigate the drive. When he got to the road, he glanced back. Through the rain, he made out a vehicle parked across his driveway. If he'd left his home through traditional means, he'd have been trapped.

A tactic he would have chosen.

Peter steered left onto the pavement and after the first curve, flipped on his headlights. It was all he could do not to press the accelerator to the floor and hightail it out of there. The question was—to where?

He glanced in the rearview mirror. He thought he'd be safe here. Have time to think. Or maybe when he didn't go to the cops right away, the assassin would stop coming after him. And Peter could reinvent himself again.

But no. After one month, the man who haunted his dreams appeared outside his cabin. He touched his right ear. Either he was lucky or the man was toying with him—intending to finish him off after he had Peter by the throat. Twice he'd escaped him. Mr. Snake Eyes was not going to be a happy guy.

Peter had to disappear completely, and he needed help planning and executing his next move. Who could he turn to? One name came to mind. He wasn't sure where to find him, but he knew someone who did. Peter pulled up the map in his head and steered his truck for Pleasant Valley, Ohio. Another bridge over another river.

9

Viktor Liska lowered his menu. Sunlight poked through the leafy canopy and danced over the tables. He missed Europe, where he dined *al fresco* in some of the greatest cities in the world. The patio at his favorite restaurant in Chicago would have to do. He gave the young waitress a brief smile as she set a cup of coffee before him.

She lingered by his table. "Is there anything else I can do for you?"

"No, thank you. This looks wonderful." He modulated his voice so his words flowed over her like honey. She trembled. He enjoyed witnessing the effect his dark good looks and aura of controlled power had on others.

As he waited for his compatriot to show, Viktor scanned the people on the busy street for anyone who didn't fit in. In his line of work, he couldn't be too careful. A man approached from his right. Viktor slid his hand into his jacket pocket but remained seated.

"Sorry. I had to park two blocks away." The balding man wiped his brow with a handkerchief.

The waitress appeared at their table and glanced at Viktor

before turning her attention to the man. "What can I get you, sir?"

The man picked up a menu with one hand and loosened his stained tie with the other. "Gee. I don't know."

Viktor eyed his companion's wrinkled shirt frayed at the cuffs and sighed.

"He will have a coffee. Black. And bring us a plate of those amazing Italian pastries." This time Viktor smiled wide, showing off all his beautiful new caps. He only hoped she wouldn't faint.

After she left, the man pulled out a small notebook.

Viktor placed a finger on the journal. "We wait until she brings our food. It will not be long." The waitress would want to see him again, but it was time to end their flirtation. Time for business.

She presented the plate of Italian confections as if setting them before a king. "I picked out the best ones for you."

"Thank you." He lowered his sunglasses and gave her a piercing look. "My colleague and I have business to conduct and do not want to be disturbed." As joy bled from her eyes, Viktor averted his gaze. Was he getting soft?

"Of course." She strode away.

"A little harsh, don't you think?" the man said.

Viktor stiffened. "What do you have to report?"

The man flipped open his notebook. "I searched his cab, but there was nothing there. I had a harder time with his apartment. The police were there. I had to climb the fire escape."

"And?"

"He'd cleared out—just like you said. The floor was torn up. Probably where he kept passports, money, and other stuff."

Viktor reached for a pastry. "What else?"

"He went to a cabin in Kentucky."

"A cabin. Of course." He tapped the table.

"Yeah. He wasn't there." The man coughed. "Somebody else got there ahead of us."

Viktor skewered the man with his eyes. "You know this how?"

"Signs of a truck getting stuck in the mud at the end of the drive—"

"Someone could have used his drive to turn around." Liska inclined his head. "I hope you have more evidence than muddy tracks."

"The kitchen window had a bullet hole in it." The man hurried on to say. "And there was blood in the sink."

"What else?"

"We're pretty sure he escaped. We found out how he got away. Pretty smart. He—"

Viktor waved a hand. "I am not interested in the details. Just tell me, do you believe he is still alive?"

"Yes."

"I see." So, someone else was after Grace. And they were one step ahead of him. That would never do.

"You do know how important this is to me, yes?" Viktor stared at his companion.

The man paled.

"Yes, boss. I'm on it."

"I'm sure you are." Viktor nibbled one edge of his pastry. "What is he driving?"

The man flipped back a few pages. "We think he's driving a truck registered in his grandfather's name."

Viktor finished chewing. "Try one of these. They're delicious." He wiped his hands on a napkin. "We have friends in the police, yes?"

"Of course."

"Find the car."

"Truck."

Viktor glared at the man. "Car, truck—you know what I mean."

The man gulped. "Yes, sir."

"I do not want him killed. I want to speak with him face-to-face." Viktor leaned closer. "Do I make myself clear about this?"

"Crystal."

"What is meant by crystal?" Viktor frowned. "A simple yes will do."

"Yes."

"Now eat a cannoli. I will call our waitress over to refill our coffees and apologize." After all, this was his favorite restaurant and maybe it was time for a change. Retirement?

10

Madison Long Zuberi sat nestled against Captain Nate Zuberi with a big bowl of popcorn in her lap. As far as she was concerned, the evening couldn't be more perfect. A fire in the fireplace, a *Forensic Files* marathon on TV, and her husband to share it.

Their dog, Oscar, was the only one whose eyes weren't glued to the screen. Instead, he raised and lowered his great head keeping track of each bite Madison and Nate took. Fortunately for him, Nate was not as strict as his mistress about feeding dogs table food—so the occasional kernel slipped from his hand and disappeared before it could touch the floor. Madison pretended not to notice.

The theme from *Mission Impossible* sounded in the middle of the program. Nate fumbled for his phone in his shirt pocket while Madison hit pause on the remote.

"Captain Zuberi ... Jeannie, hi ...What?" Nate's elbow caught Madison on the head as he jumped to his feet.

"Ow." She rubbed her left temple.

"Sorry." He patted her head. "What did you say?" He

35

tripped over Oscar who yelped and sprung to his feet, knocking the popcorn bowl out of Madison's lap. Nate cringed and mouthed sorry again as he crunched his way into the kitchen.

"Is he in jail? Is the other guy pressing charges?" Nate's voice rose then he apparently listened. "Okay. I'm coming over ... Yes, I think it's the best thing to do. I'll see you as soon as I can get there." Nate turned to Madison and sighed heavily. "Jeannie's son, Tommy, is in jail in Cincinnati, and Bill is out of town." He took Madison's hand. "I feel like I need to be there for her because ... well, you know."

"I understand." Madison walked him to the door. "Go. Let me know what's going on. Okay?"

"I will." Nate pulled her into a kiss. "I love you."

"I know." She smiled at him. "Now go."

Tommy. Again. Last month—no, two weeks ago—he wrecked his car. Bill was on a business trip. Nate helped her then too. Madison didn't mind. Jeannie was a friend, but she worried about Tommy and who he hung around with these days. Especially since Bill's new job involved more travel, and Jeannie was left to parent a teenager alone.

She stepped off the front porch onto the lawn. Tilting her head back, she marveled at all the stars shining brightly in the crisp autumn night. One of many advantages to living on the lake away from the city. Very little light pollution. She took a deep breath and brought her gaze back to earth. A strange gray pickup sat in her neighbor's driveway. Sarah hadn't mentioned any company coming. Huh.

Wonder who it is?

Madison glanced at her watch—8:15. Every light was on at Sarah and Ed Hall's house next door, and she had a bad case of the nosys. Should she or shouldn't she? Why not? After all, she was just checking to make sure her friends were okay, the neighborly thing to do.

She strode across the lawn and rapped on the door. A man

answered, but it wasn't Ed. This man didn't look anything like a history professor in his seventies.

The man in the doorway wore blue jeans that fit like they were tailored and a crisp white shirt with the tails hanging out. His blue eyes twinkled over full lips parted in a smile showing amazing white teeth resembling a young Brad Pitt.

"Rafe. What are you doing here?" She waved a hand. "Sorry. That didn't come out right. This is your aunt and uncle's house. I meant ..."

He chuckled. "Come in, Madison."

"Did you get a new truck?"

"No. It belongs to a friend of mine. Come meet him."

"I don't want to intrude." She backed up a step. "I wanted to check on your aunt and uncle."

"Right." He laughed and grabbed her arm. "Admit it. You were being nosy."

"I was not." Her face grew hot.

"Come on. I was going to introduce you anyway. He'll be living in the house next to you for a while."

"Warren's old house?"

Rafe nodded. "I rented it for a few months."

A hint of his woody cologne tickled her nose as she followed him into the family room.

"Darlin'." Sarah jumped to her feet. "Would ye like something to drink?"

Madison inspected her friend's face. What was going on? Sarah's heightened Irish brogue indicated her stress.

"Sure. Hot tea? Do you need some help?"

"Nay, nay. Sit yerself down."

Madison surveyed the room. "Evening, Ed."

He smiled at her, lips drawn together tightly.

Definitely something up. Her eyes eventually landed on the stranger. She never thought of Rafe as having friends. In the two years plus she'd known and worked with him, he'd never talked about his personal life.

"This is Paul Gray," Rafe said. "He's in a bit of trouble and needs our help."

"*Our* help?" She jerked her head to stare at her boss.

"Yes." His twinkling eyes had grown hard. "Don't worry. All I need from you is not to say a thing to anyone about him. Including your police captain husband. Okay?"

"Has he done something illegal? Are we harboring a fugitive?"

"No. All you need to know. Trust me. It's for your own good."

"Oh, great. When I signed on with you, you didn't say anything about—" She swept her hand in Gray's direction. "Rafe, I don't work well in the dark. I need to know what's going on here."

He studied her. "You're right. But now's not the time. Let's get Paul settled, and we'll talk more."

"No offense." She faced the stranger. "But I don't know you from Al Capone. Probably a bad choice of words, but you know what I mean."

"None taken." He shook his head. "I'd be wary too if I were you."

His voice was soft, and he sounded weary—like he'd been on a long journey. She eyed his worn hiking boots planted firmly apart, his dark green cargo pants smeared with dirt, and the dingy gray T-shirt. He raised his head, and she was startled by alert dark gray eyes.

Then she noticed the scar. A white ridge cutting across his left cheek from his hairline to his upper lip. He gave her a small smile and she averted her gaze.

11

Peter lowered his head. He'd seen the surge of pity in her eyes. This was not how he'd planned it. These people weren't supposed to be involved. What was he thinking? He'd located Rafe and approached him for help. Next thing he knew, he was here. Meeting the older couple and this woman Madison. He must impress upon Rafe just how dangerous the assassin …

"We need to talk." He peered at Rafe. "Privately."

The two men stepped onto the deck at the rear of the house. A breeze ruffled the surface of the lake, and the moon's reflection broke into a thousand pieces. Leaves rustled in the trees, and somewhere close, wind chimes added their musical tones.

"It's nice here," Peter said.

"Yep."

"But you had no business involving your aunt and uncle and Madison." Peter faced Rafe. "This guy is dangerous. He isn't going to stop until he kills me. And he doesn't care who he eliminates along the way."

"I get it. But he has to find you first. And then he has to get through me."

"All he has to do is threaten to hurt someone you love." Peter pointed through the sliding glass door.

"I can take care of them."

"You'd better—because I don't want their deaths on my conscience." Peter poked his finger on Rafe's chest. "I came to you for help to stop this guy *before* more innocent people were killed. Now I feel like I've put your family and friend in his crosshairs. I don't like it one bit." He glanced at the sliding glass door and locked eyes with the intense amber gaze of Madison Long. How much had she overheard?

"I NEED TO GET GOING," Madison said. "Oscar will be wondering if I'm coming home."

"Who's Oscar? Your husband?" Peter said.

"No. He's my dog." She turned to hug Sarah and Ed, then joined the men on the deck. "See you tomorrow."

"Wait. We'll walk with you," Rafe said. "I need to get Paul settled in the rental."

She stopped short and put her hands on her hips. "Give me a break. I know his name's not Paul Gray."

"It is now." Rafe stared into her eyes and hissed softly. "Understood?"

She lowered her hands and nodded. He'd never talked to her like that. Boss or no boss, she didn't like it. They needed to get a few things straight if she was to remain in his employ. But not tonight. Too late and too tired. A talk like that required a clear head. Besides, Rafe promised to tell her what was going on after his friend was settled. Their talk tomorrow would probably take care of all her questions and misunderstandings.

"Goodnight, gentlemen." She veered to the right and approached the front of her house. To her surprise, Rafe caught her just as she was about to turn the knob.

"Hang on," he said. "Sorry for being abrupt back there."

"No problem." She shrugged. They'd still have that talk.

"I know you, Madison."

She raised her eyes to his. Rafe had become like a second brother to her. It made things difficult at times—a brother and her boss.

"You're upset with me, and I'm going to get an earful tomorrow, but it's okay. I deserve it. And we will talk more about what's going on. For now, you'll have to trust me. What I do, I do to keep you and my aunt and uncle safe. Okay?"

She nodded. She trusted Rafe. But then her mind filled with Nate's face. She wouldn't keep secrets from her husband. Even if it meant losing her job and her friend. They'd have that talk tomorrow. "Goodnight, boss."

He jogged to where Peter waited in the shadows.

WHEN RAFE and Madison walked to her front door, Peter positioned his back against a tree. He needed to stay alert—frosty, as they said in the Army. He touched his damaged right earlobe. A little to the left and ... Maybe those three oaks had protected him somehow after all.

"Ready to see your new digs?" Rafe said.

Peter nodded.

"After we check it out, I'll drive your truck down and park it in the garage." Rafe unlocked the front door. "If you need to go anywhere, I can drive you."

As Peter walked down the long hall to the large open room at the back, he took mental notes of the first floor. With the wall of windows and glass doors overlooking the lake, there were too many entry points. And he hadn't even seen the second floor yet. This place would be hard to defend.

"What do you think?" Rafe gazed around the empty space.

"Not bad. I should only need about five guys to secure it properly."

Rafe sighed. "Yeah. Well. Hopefully, security won't be something we need to worry about. We'll have to get you some furniture."

"I won't need much. Just a folding table and chair. A cot." Peter wandered into the kitchen. "Some cooking stuff."

"Man, you sure are easy to please." Rafe chuckled.

"I don't want any attention drawn to myself." Peter swiveled around. "Nothing that will get the neighbors talking. Seriously, what about security?"

"I've done this before." Rafe's eyes sharpened. "We'll move everything in quickly and quietly after dark. We'll install cameras outside and in, along with motion sensors, and the alarm system will go directly to me."

Peter felt hopeful for the first time since leaving Kentucky.

"We've got a lot to talk about, but first you need some rest. You should be good here tonight, and I'll be back first thing in the morning." Rafe motioned to his right. "Madison is next door if you need anything, and my aunt and uncle are in the house beyond. So, you've got people here."

You've got people here. How long had it been since he'd heard that?

12

Peter spied Madison sitting cross-legged at the end of her pier. Her dog splashed in the lake nearby, immersed in some doggy game involving a ball and a lot of woofing. She appeared to be meditating, but as he drew closer, he realized something wasn't quite right. She seemed taller somehow.

"Good morning. I hope—"

The statuesque woman leaped to her feet, yanking a collapsible baton from the pocket of her purple camo pants.

Peter threw his hands up in a gesture of surrender and backed slowly off the dock. "Sorry. I didn't mean to startle you."

"What do you mean creeping up on a person?" She stepped toward him.

"I wasn't creeping. I just walk quiet." He shrugged.

She glared at him.

The dog bounced out of the lake and shook himself dry with such vigor the spray doused everything within twenty feet—including the woman and Peter. Satisfied, he trotted over to Peter, dropped his ball at Peter's feet, and wagged his tail.

"Oscar seems to like you." She retracted her baton but held it at the ready.

Violet eyes. He'd never seen eyes that color before.

43

"Well? Are you going to tell me who you are?"

He blinked. "Sorry. I'm Paul Gray. I'm renting the house next door."

"I see."

He bent to rub Oscar behind his ears but kept his attention on her. "What's your name?"

"Zoe Poole. I'm a friend of Madison." She lifted her chin toward the house. "And I work with her."

Peter stood. "Then you know Rafe. He's a friend of mine. We were in Afghanistan together."

She studied him. After a moment, she strode past him in the direction of the house. "Have you had breakfast?"

"No, but I wouldn't want to put you out."

She rounded on him. "I wouldn't ask you to breakfast if I didn't want to."

"Technically, you didn't ask me to breakfast. You just asked if I'd had breakfast."

"Don't be difficult. You know what I meant." She shook her head. "Come on."

"Yes ma'am."

"And don't call me ma'am." She pounded onto the deck and threw open the door. "Madison, there's one more for breakfast."

The aromas of frying bacon, eggs, and toast surrounded him, and he wiped a hand across his mouth to catch any drool. But he couldn't control the audible grumble from his gut.

MADISON EYED HER GUEST. Paul ate like he hadn't eaten for months, shoveling eggs into his mouth with a soup spoon. And the bacon. He ate a whole pound by himself.

Oscar sat next to him, a look of doggie amazement on his face.

At last, Paul sat back in his chair and burped.

"Would you like some toast?"

"No." He frowned. "I don't think so."

"Good. I only have half a loaf of bread left."

"Hey." He smiled. "Your friend asked me to breakfast."

"I'm only glad I didn't offer to treat you at a restaurant," Zoe said.

"Treat who at a restaurant?" Nate stood in the doorway.

Madison glanced at Zoe. How could she explain the strange man in her kitchen when she herself knew so little about him? She'd hoped to speak to Rafe before telling Nate about Paul—or whoever he was. She jumped from her chair and ran to Nate.

"Sweetheart." She wrapped her arms around his neck and kissed him.

Obviously distracted, Nate kissed her back, but he gently pulled away and focused on Paul.

"Hi." The man rose and extended his hand. "I'm Rafe's friend, Paul Gray. I'm renting next door and don't have all my things yet." He gestured toward the table. "Madison and Zoe graciously asked me to breakfast this morning. I guess I was hungrier than I thought."

"Nate Zuberi. Nice to meet you. I—"

"He's the police captain." Madison patted his chest. "A very good one." Her palms were sweating. Best to get Nate on his way. She'd tell him all about Paul later. Once she knew the whole story herself.

"Are you okay?" Nate quirked an eyebrow.

"Sure. Why wouldn't I be?"

He pecked her on the cheek. "Got to run." He turned to Peter. "You'll have to come for dinner some time so we can get acquainted."

"Yes, he will." Madison turned him toward the door.

"Are you sure you're all right?"

"I'm fine. Let me walk you out."

On the porch, Nate pulled her into his arms. "What's going on? You're nervous. Does this guy spook you? Do I need to stick around?"

"No." She brushed lint from his lapel. "He's a nice guy. And besides, Zoe's here. I didn't sleep well." She smiled at him. "See you for dinner?"

"I need to go back to Cincinnati." He paused. "You understand."

She did, but she didn't have to like it.

"I'll call later." He drew her in for a kiss, his hands warm and strong against her back. "I love you."

"I love you too." She felt the familiar ache in her chest as she watched him drive away.

Madison sighed and returned to the kitchen. Paul washed dishes at the sink.

"What are you doing? I have a dishwasher."

He swiveled at the waist to face her. "You're welcome."

Madison's face grew hot. "Sorry. I'm not myself this morning."

"No problem." Paul dried his hands. "Thanks for the grub. It was great."

Oscar scrambled to his feet, a woof sounding low in his chest.

Someone was at the door. "Back up, dog." She pushed her big lab to the side and put an eye to the peephole. Rafe. He had some explaining to do.

"Good morning." He strolled in. "Is Paul here?"

"In the kitchen." She hesitated a minute her hand curling into a fist. Tempting.

"I need you to go outside, Zoe."

She threw him a salute and motioned to Oscar. "Come on, big boy. Let's go play."

Rafe fixed his gaze on his friend. "Glad to find you here. I want you to give a description of the assassin to Madison. She's a good artist. We can use her sketch to search the database."

"I'm not drawing any pictures for you until you fill me in." She glared at him. "Nate was just here, and it was awful. A strange man in our house."

Paul glanced at Rafe who gave him a slight nod. He leaned against the counter.

"I WAS SITTING at my desk in Afghanistan reading some reports when a couple of guys stopped outside my window against the side of the building," Peter said. "It's funny how people will stand next to an open window, and just because there's nobody in sight feel like they're alone."

"They began talking about all the money they were making off the government hauling freight." He laughed. "I guess they thought even if there was someone listening, they wouldn't understand. They were wrong. I speak fluent Pashto."

"What did you do?" Madison said.

"I did what I do best—I investigated. But oddly enough, I couldn't find anything. Until one day, I discovered a memo left inside a file by accident. It led me to other files. They gave me enough reason to suspect our freight handler in Afghanistan was using U.S. money to pay off the Taliban and enemy warlords for safe passage through their territories."

"What's so bad about that? They needed to be able to get through, right?"

"Yes, but by paying them with U.S. funds, we ended up financially supporting our own enemies." Peter sighed. "Not good. They also lied about the money paid to friendly warlords and pocketed the difference. Many of them became very rich. I knew my friend, Lawrence Merton, had the contract for Afghanistan. He would have been the one hiring the local freight company. I decided—like a fool—to tell him about the fraud first instead of my superior officer." Peter took a drink of water.

"I thought he'd be outraged—and he acted like he was—at first. But then—" Anger surged through him at the memory. "Some local thugs visited me. They threatened my grandparents and told me money had been deposited in my account. If I didn't forget about what I knew, not only would they implicate me, they'd kill my family."

"How awful." Madison fingered the silver cross at her neck.

"I called Lawrence expecting him to help me out, but all he said was I'd better do what they asked. I knew then they'd got to him too. I haven't spoken to him since." He couldn't bear to see the pity in her eyes.

"Don't feel sorry for me. I left the Army, moved back to St. Louis, and used the money to buy a cab." He straightened his shoulders. "Now you know what kind of man you're harboring. I'll have to live with the shame for the rest of my life."

"Yes. A man who puts the welfare of his family above all else," she said. "What you did wasn't shameful. It was human."

"I agree. He did what he had to do," Rafe said. "Can we move on now?"

"So, Paul Gray is really Peter Grace." Madison slowly shook her head. "That's not going to fool anybody." She stepped closer to her boss. "And we need to keep Zoe in the loop."

"I suppose so. But we can't use his real name. There can be no slips." A grim expression etched Rafe's face.

Madison pulled Zoe away from a game of fetch with Oscar. "You're needed inside." She relayed to Zoe the truth about Peter.

"Peter? I thought his name was Paul."

"I told you." Madison sat next to Rafe. "Bad idea."

Rafe narrowed his eyes at her. "It's easier to remember a name with similar letters to your real name."

"Baloney." Madison faced him. "You're just making it more confusing."

Rafe scooted closer to her. "What alias would you have given him? John Smith?"

She tapped the table in front of him. "If he's in hiding, why does he need an alias at all? Explain that one to me."

Peter rose and moved by Zoe. "Do they always argue this way?"

Zoe sighed. "Pretty much. You'd think they were brother and

sister. I just let them run out of steam." She cocked her head at him. "What *is* your real name?"

"I'm Peter Grace." He smiled at her and stuck out his hand. "Nice to meet you, Zoe."

She took it and smirked. "Same here."

He held onto her hand and rotated her arm to reveal a delicate tattoo. A feather with Psalm 91:4 inked inside.

"He will cover you with his feathers. He will shelter you with his wings." She pulled her hand back and touched the design on her right forearm.

Someday he would show her his tattoo of wings on his chest containing a similar biblical address. Wonder what else he had in common with this remarkable woman?

"When you two are done getting acquainted, you might as well tell her the rest of the story." Rafe indicated for them to join him and Madison.

"Is it safe?" Peter eyed them.

"Yes. Madison won as usual."

Peter's third time through and it still sounded unreal to him —like words in a novel. After he'd finished, Zoe brought him a bottle of sparkling water. Peter raised an eyebrow.

"No?"

"No," he said. "Coffee please. Black."

"You do know what caffeine does to your body?" She frowned at him.

"Keeps it humming like a well-oiled machine."

"Well, you'll need to get your own lubricant. I'll not be party to the destruction of someone else's health." Zoe pulled out a chair at the kitchen table. "As for changing Peter to Paul, I mean, what good does that really do? And the same last initial as well? No self-respecting bad guy will be fooled. Sorry."

"Exactly what I told Rafe." Madison crossed her arms in front of her.

"I'm used to finding people. Not hiding them." Rafe threw

up his hands in surrender. "Next time—if there is a next time—I'll let someone else pick the alias."

"Besides, you and Rafe were friends back when, right? If the men who are after you are as good as you say, they'll find out and be here in a heartbeat searching for you. I mean they found you in the Kentucky backwoods. How hard will it be to find you in Pleasant Valley, Ohio?"

Quiet descended on the kitchen as all eyes honed in on Zoe.

"I've made a terrible mistake. Now I've put all of your lives in danger." Peter pushed away from the table. "I need to move on."

Rafe grabbed his arm. "That won't solve anything. The assassin can't take any chances. We could know everything you know. The outcome's the same." He released his grip. "You came to me for help. We're all in this now. Are you willing to help us?"

Peter contemplated the open honest faces of the people sitting around the table. Strangers willing to risk their lives for him. Would he do the same for them? Even Rafe. Peter hadn't seen him for years, but when he called, there was no hesitation. A nod was all he could manage.

"We need a plan." Rafe turned to face the group. "I'll move in with Peter. Zoe, can you live with my aunt and uncle for a time? Madison, you should be fine here with Oscar and Nate."

13

Peter watched Zoe grab another sparkling water from the refrigerator and turn, catching his gaze before he could look away. The corners of her mouth lifted in a smile that did more for him than a slug of caffeine. She passed behind him to take a seat at the table, trailing a scent of fresh air and grass.

"I'll be happy to move in with Sarah and Ed." She took a swig of her water. "What's on the agenda in the meantime?" She pulled her phone from a pocket in her purple camo vest.

Something was wrong. Her violet eyes darkened.

"I need to leave for a couple hours, boss." Zoe walked to the door.

"Hang on," Rafe said. "Why? What's going on?"

"It's my mom." Her shoulders sagged. "She's in a senior care facility in Cincinnati. They texted. I need to go."

"Do you want me to go with you?" Madison grabbed her sweater.

"No." Zoe put up a hand. "Thanks." She tossed her a brief smile.

And then she was gone.

Rafe wheeled to face Madison. "Did you know about her mother?"

"No. You're her boss. If anyone should know her background, it's you."

"Nobody tells me anything." He paced the kitchen. "She's your friend."

"Hey, you two." Peter stood. "Apparently, Zoe didn't want either of you to know for whatever reason."

"She should have confided in us," Rafe said. "We would have helped."

"I pray her mother's okay." Madison's hand went to the cross at her throat.

Peter put his hand in his pocket and cupped his mother's necklace in his fingers. For Zoe's sake, he prayed she had strength to face whatever lay ahead.

ZOE STEERED her bright blue SUV onto the road she'd come to know too well. She'd intended to tell her friends about her mother someday. But on her terms and her timing. Uncle Harry and his desperation had ruined that for her. Just like his gambling habit had ruined so many other things.

Screams spilled from her mouth into the car interior until she'd rid herself of the demons of frustration and anger that threatened to overwhelm her. Some called it scream therapy. She called it releasing negative energy. Now cleansed, she was ready to approach things the way she should.

Uncle Harry, her mother's brother, had shown up at the facility today looking for his sister. No doubt in another attempt to steal her share of their inheritance. Zoe had left strict instructions not to admit him. Or to give him any information about her mother—whether she was a resident there or not. They had kept their promise.

But he knew.

The question now was what should Zoe do about it? She could move her mother somewhere else, but there weren't many places with the level of care she needed. And this facility had been a blessing from day one.

She hated the thought of moving.

A parking space opened up in the front circle, and Zoe snagged it. Walking into the foyer always made her grin. If she didn't know better, she'd think it was a swanky resort. Plush carpet. Comfy seating areas. Rich colors. Even a crystal chandelier.

The woman at the desk recognized her. "We did what you said, Ms. Poole." Audrey, as her nametag announced, clasped her hands tightly at her waist.

"I'm sure you did." Zoe smiled at her. "Thank you. Tell me what he said as much as you can remember."

She put a finger to her chin. "First, he said he wanted to visit Mrs. Poole. When I told him we had no guest by that name, he smirked and said, 'No, of course not.' Then he left."

"He didn't give you a name?"

"I asked as he was leaving, but he ignored me."

"What did he look like?"

Audrey's description fit Harry to a *T*. He was testing the waters. But why? What would be his next move?

"Did you happen to see his car?"

"Right after he left, a silver sporty car zoomed out of the parking lot. That may have been him."

"Hopefully, he won't be back. But if he is, just let me know." Zoe cast a glance down the hall. "I'll see mother while I'm here. Okay?"

"Of course." The woman beamed. "She'll be glad to see you."

Possibly. But would she know who Zoe was? Depended on the day.

ON THE DRIVE BACK, Zoe made up her mind. She refused to let Uncle Harry force her into moving away from a job and friends she'd grown to love. Three hours later, Zoe pulled into Madison's driveway.

Her long legs ate up the distance around the house to the back deck. She hesitated at the slider going into the kitchen, her resolve wavering. Maybe she could leave Uncle Harry out of it. So, he'd found her and her mom? Zoe had known it was just a matter of time. What could he really do anyway?

She gazed through the glass door to where Rafe and Madison appeared to be preoccupied with something at the kitchen window. Her friends—no—her family. She blinked away her tears and opened the door.

"WHAT ARE YOU TWO DOING?" Peter had a hard time concentrating, his senses alert to any indication that Zoe had returned.

"There's some faint imprints on the original sheet of paper you found." Rafe held the sheet up to the window. "Madison's going to work with it in the lab downstairs."

And there she was.

"Zoe, you're back." Madison grabbed her in a hug. "How's your mom?"

"She's good. False alarm." Zoe backed out of Madison's embrace. "I'm sorry I ..."

"We'll talk later," Rafe said. "We've got work to do."

Peter locked eyes with Zoe. "Glad you're back and everything's okay." But was she okay? He hadn't known her long, but something felt different about her. Maybe because she'd been forced to reveal something about her private life she didn't want to share? Or was there more to it?

Peter and Zoe moved in behind Rafe. Their arms brushed, and for a split second he lost concentration.

"What did you find?" Zoe said.

"The shadow image of a phone number and possibly a name.

But we won't be sure until she does the tests." He handed the paper to Madison. "See what you can find."

"What about me? What can I do?" Zoe said.

"You're going to help me install cameras and alarms."

"Great. Where do we begin?"

"We'll assess what equipment we need, and then you'll make a trip into town to pick it up." Rafe handed her a credit card. "I'll text you the address."

"Maybe I should go with ..." Peter's words crashed and burned against the look on his friend's face. He took a step back.

"What part of in hiding don't you get, pal?" Rafe matched Peter's stride with one of his own.

"I came to you for help ... pal." Anger erupted from deep inside. "Not to be treated like a prisoner." While Peter stood a head taller than the private investigator, Peter was not as muscular.

"Good grief." Zoe put two hands between them and pushed them apart. "I thought you guys were friends—and grown-ups."

Once again, the voice of reason.

"Sorry." Peter stuck out his hand. "I know you're just trying to help me."

Rafe grabbed his hand and pulled him into a bear hug. "Me too. I can be a control freak."

"Can I trust you two to play nice now?" Zoe's violet eyes danced with glee.

Whatever difference he thought he saw had vanished. The Zoe he first met was with them again.

"Madison can act as referee." Rafe scanned the kitchen. "Where is she?"

Zoe nodded out the kitchen window toward the lake.

14

Madison pulled Oscar closer to her. "What a fine mess I've gotten myself into this time, Oscar." She swished her feet through the water. Spring fed, Lake Pleasant stayed cold most of the year, but the rains in autumn served to warm the top water a bit. That didn't help the bite in the air.

Madison shivered. "Actually, I didn't get myself into this mess. Rafe did."

Oscar's tail thumped at the mention of Rafe's name.

"I know. He's your good buddy, but he sure can be frustrating." She smoothed his fur. "The big question is, how do I tell Nate about all this? He's not going to like it."

Oscar pressed a wet nose to her cheek.

"What if he wants me to quit my job?" She hugged her Labrador around the neck. "I love my work. But I love my husband more."

She grabbed her sweet dog by the loose skin around his jowls and turned his face to hers.

"What do you think? Will Nate make me choose?"

Oscar licked her nose.

"I don't know either." Madison rose and brushed off the seat of her jeans. "Back to the house, boy. We've got work to do."

Zoe met Madison and Oscar halfway up the lawn. "Thought I'd come check on you. I'm getting some things from my place and then into town."

"Right. The security equipment."

"Are you okay?"

"I'm upset we've ended up in someone's crosshairs." Madison threw Oscar's ball and watched him lope after it. "It's not Rafe's fault. And I don't think Peter intended for this to happen. But I've been through this once before, and I'm not happy about being in this situation again."

"Neither am I."

"What do you mean?" Madison searched her friend's face.

"I'll tell you about it sometime, but now I really need to go."

ZOE SLOWED on the concrete span crossing the water, her initial view of the burbling stream that ran by her cabin. She stopped, unlocked the gate blocking further access up the dirt road, and drove through. Majestic pine trees, a gurgling brook, and a two-bedroom log cabin with a screened porch entrance. A barn sat back and to one side. All sheltered from view of the road by trees and undergrowth.

She'd fallen in love with this property at first sight. Who wouldn't? Her little piece of heaven.

"Hi, guys." Zoe bent and stuck her hand out as two gray foxes approached. "You been keeping the varmints away?"

The bigger of the two touched his nose to her palm. They looked good. So much better than they had when she rescued them from their den six months ago. The vision of their mother bleeding on the side of the road brought tears to her eyes. Zoe couldn't save her, but the local vet showed Zoe how to care for the cubs.

And release them back into nature—where they belonged. One of the hardest things she'd ever done.

"I'll bring you a treat before I leave."

She stepped inside to her bedroom and packed a suitcase. Should she throw in something besides camo? Maybe a couple pair of jeans and some shirts. Her phone vibrated on her hip. A number she didn't recognize. She answered.

"Zoe? It's been a long time. How's my favorite niece?" Uncle Harry's voice slithered over her phone like a snake invading her Eden.

"How did you get this number?" Her eyes were drawn to her tattoo. *His faithful promises are your armor and protection.*

"Money can get you a lot of things."

With Harry, everything revolved around money. And how he could get more of it without lifting a finger. That's where her mom came in.

"What do you want?"

"Want?"

His tone suggested hurt feelings, but she knew better.

"I just want to be a family again," he said. "Have dinner with me and we can talk."

"I can't. You caught me at a busy time. Maybe later." She grabbed a pen and paper. "Where are you? I'll call when I'm free." Always good to keep an eye on the nest of vipers.

"I'm leaving tomorrow. I have a board meeting in Pittsburgh to attend." He paused. "Are you sure you can't free up some time for your Uncle Harry tonight?"

"Sorry." She let the silence drag.

"Well. I tried." His icy tone closed around her throat like fingers. "Remember what I said." The line went dead.

What was he up to?

After alerting the staff at her mom's care home, Zoe packed her car and secured her house. She grabbed some grapes from the fridge on her way out and sat on the bottom step holding a purple orb between her fingers.

Noses twitched and dark eyes flitted between her and the offering she held out for them.

"I promised you a treat," Zoe said softly. "Come."

As usual, the larger animal closed the distance first. He gently took the proffered grape and quickly backed away. Zoe replaced it with another. This time the female came forward.

"Hello, sweet lady."

Black eyes swiveled up as the female fox curled her lips back to grasp the grape without touching Zoe's fingers.

After several such encounters, the foxes stayed close to Zoe as she offered grape after grape. A big step in their relationship. Maybe one day they would trust her enough to let her pet them. But not today.

On the drive to the store in town, she saw no sign of a silver sports car or anything else suspicious.

Everything went without a hitch. Zoe found the shop, and the equipment had been set aside for her. They even carried it out to her car. Mission accomplished. Now she was headed back to the lake.

"Be there in about ten minutes." She pushed hang up on her steering wheel and slowed at the four-way stop.

Cars and trucks took turns passing through the intersection. By the time she sat before the stop sign, no other vehicles waited at the crossing. She pressed the accelerator. A large black object filled her peripheral vision on the left. She stomped the accelerator, and her little SUV responded.

But not fast enough.

The truck rammed her behind the driver's door sending her car spinning across the pavement. She jarred to a stop against a lamppost. Revolver at the ready, she unbuckled, slid out on the passenger side, and advanced on the pickup.

Empty. The driver had fled. But not without injury. Blood glistened on the steering wheel. Zoe holstered her weapon and took out her phone. She snapped photos, took a sample of the smear, and used tape to grab some fingerprints.

People gathered and sirens blared in the distance. She surveyed the crowd for anyone with an injured forehead.

If this was just an accident, why did the driver take off? Too many tickets? Drunk?

Or was this intentional? Related to Peter?

Or to her?

"I'VE BEEN IN AN ACCIDENT." Zoe held her phone with one hand and the ice pack on her knee with the other. "Can one of you come get me?"

"Are you hurt?" Madison said.

"Nothing serious. I banged my knee on the steering wheel."

"I'll be right there."

"Madison, could you come alone? I'm not up to Rafe and his questions right now."

"No problem."

About twelve minutes later, Madison's small silver hybrid pulled quietly onto the shoulder. "Need a ride, lady?"

"Thanks." Zoe stowed her stuff and the equipment from the store in the back and dropped into the front seat next to her friend.

"You want to talk about it?"

"Not right now, but I do have some things I need you to analyze." She threw a brief look at Madison.

"Okay, but eventually I'll want to know what this is all about. Deal?"

"Deal." Zoe could live with that. Who knows? Eventually may never happen.

15

"Good morning, Captain Zuberi." Madison snuggled against her husband. She loved early mornings before the alarm started the day.

Nate pulled her close and kissed the top of her head. "What are your plans for today, Mrs. Zuberi?"

Mrs. Zuberi. A smile started at her mouth and traveled all the way to her toes bringing a sigh of contentment with it.

"I think it's time for a second honeymoon." She rubbed his chest.

He laughed. "We've only been married a year."

"I know, but it was so wonderful having you all to myself. No other obligations, no cases to solve, no friends of your boss to take care of ..." She rolled over on her back and frowned at the ceiling.

He turned toward her. "Are you upset because I've been going to Cincinnati to help Jeannie's son?"

"No." She swiveled her head to face him. "Jeannie's my friend too. I want you to help her in any way you can."

"Is something going on with Rafe and this new guy, Paul?"

"Sort of." She sat up. He needed to know everything. But how would he react? "It's a long story. First of all, his name's not

Paul. It's Peter." Madison touched her husband's arm. "Promise you'll listen before going ballistic."

After she finished, Nate scrubbed his face with his hands. "I'm not sure whether to strangle Rafe for putting you in the middle of this or quit my job so I can be your full-time bodyguard."

"Neither." She spoke with as much confidence as she could muster. "You have a job to do, and so do I. I'll be fine." Throwing off the covers, she hopped out of bed. "So, let's get to it."

"Wait a minute." Nate exploded from the bed and grabbed her arm. "This is a little more than business as usual. You just told me a professional assassin could be on his way here in search of a man currently under my protection."

"Maybe. He may not discover where Peter is, or he may have decided it's not worth it."

"Not according to what Rafe or Peter thinks." Nate crossed his arms in front of his chest. "Right?"

"No." Madison lowered her eyes. "But we're working hard to identify the guy before anything happens." She pulled his arms open and moved in for a hug. "We have a plan."

He held her at arm's length. "What plan?"

"Rafe is moving in with Peter, and Zoe is bunking with Sarah and Ed while we follow up on the leads we have."

"That's it? That's your plan?" His face hardened into a scowl.

"No. Rafe is installing security equipment on all of our houses. And his men will be guarding the entrance to our subdivision." Her eyes filled with tears. "Are you angry with me?"

"Yes, I'm angry." He squeezed her arms. Pulling her into an embrace, he buried his face in her hair. "But I'm not angry with you. I'm upset with the whole situation."

"The truth is, so am I." She leaned back to look into his deep brown eyes. "But Peter and Rafe have a history. They served in Afghanistan together. Rafe couldn't say no."

"And now he's put all of us in jeopardy."

"Would you have turned him away?" She knew the answer before he said it.

"No." Nate touched the silver cross Madison always wore around her neck. "But your plan needs work. Like what if the killers come in from the lake?"

Scenes from the past of a dead man and a frightening ride across the water flashed through her mind like the trailer for a horror film, and she shuddered.

"I'm sorry." Nate kissed her lightly. "I know how hard you've tried to forget that time, but Rafe needs to prepare for a possible water attack if he hasn't already."

"I'll tell him." The light in the room grew dim as dark memories passed between her and the sun. She raised her hand to her necklace.

"Your drawing paid off." Rafe waved a handful of papers at Madison as he entered her kitchen.

"Really? We have a name for Peter's assassin?"

"Viktor Liska. The Fox." He read from a report prepared by his team.

"What kind of name is Viktor Liska?" she said.

"Czech. He's a hit man who began his career in Europe."

"Wait till Peter and Zoe get here to tell me the rest." She sat a cup of coffee in front of him. "I've got something else I want to talk to you about." How would Rafe react when he learned she'd told Nate everything? Yet another person in on the case. Rant and rave? Or fire her?

"I'm listening."

"I told Nate about Peter." She brought her mug to the table. "Needless to say, he wasn't too happy about me being in danger again."

"Does he want you to quit?" Rafe stared into his cup. "I wouldn't blame him."

"No." She narrowed her eyes at him. What was he asking her? "Do *you* want me to quit?"

"Of course not." He paced in front of the sink. "But I'm not crazy about having the police captain mad at me either."

"He's angry with the situation, not you—or me," Madison said. "But he did bring up a good point. Do we have any security against an attack from the lake?"

"He's right." Rafe went to her kitchen window. "We've got cameras aimed at the lake, but we need an early warning system. Let me think on it."

Madison joined him. The sun played hide and seek behind fluffy white clouds, making an ever-changing mosaic of light and dark on the surface of the lake. A couple walked the path with their children skipping ahead. The boy ran onto her deck to look at her canoe, but his dad called him back.

Oscar woofed and scrambled to his feet, tail wagging.

"In coming." Rafe unlocked the kitchen door for Peter and Zoe. "Peter, what do you know about trip wires and similar security devices?"

"I could help with those things," Zoe said.

Rafe frowned. "I have a feeling there's a lot you didn't put on your resume."

"I told you I worked for the Border Patrol in Texas." Zoe averted her eyes as a flush crept up her neck. "I learned a lot."

Rafe rejoined Madison at the window. "I've seen lots of people use the path in back of the houses. Is it a public walkway?"

"When I bought on the lake, I agreed the path could be used by the residents. I own the land on both sides of the lane."

"That's a problem. Is there any way we can block access from Aunt Sarah's house past the rental?"

"I don't see how."

What if they couldn't secure the lake side? What then? Madison's vision blurred. Memories from her ordeal flooded her brain. Once more, the smell of the wool balaclava her kidnapper wore filled her nostrils. Along with the scent of peppermint on his breath. The pressure of the needle at her neck. She was going to be sick.

In the bathroom, she leaned on the sink—tears threatening to spill over her eyelids. She couldn't do this again. *Lord, I need you.* She stared at the blotchy reflection in the mirror. *The Lord is my strength and my shield. My heart trusts in Him.* Her life verse. Did she believe it, or were they empty words?

He got me through the last time, and He would do the same again. She splashed water on her face, ran a comb through her hair, and opened the bathroom door.

Zoe, Peter, and Rafe stood in the hallway with anxious looks.

"Sorry. If I'd known there was a line for the bathroom, I'd have been a little quicker."

Relief flooded her friends' faces.

"I was going to ask if you're okay, but it's clear you are," Zoe said with a good Groucho Marx impersonation. Including the waggle of eyebrows.

Madison laughed. "You're too young to know about Groucho Marx." She started down the hall toward the kitchen.

"Lots of television with my mom," Zoe said.

"Who's Groucho Marx?" Rafe said behind her.

"Didn't he write a book on communism?" Peter said.

"No. That was his brother, Zeppo," Zoe chimed in.

"Stop." Tears of laughter ran down Madison's face. "Or I'll be running back to the bathroom for a different reason."

"Zoe, you and I can discuss security later." Rafe indicated for them to sit. "We've got some news."

"Rafe has discovered the name of the assassin. It's Viktor Liska. The Fox." Madison inclined her head toward Peter. "You were partially right. He's Czech, not Russian."

"You have more news for me?" Viktor Liska sipped his espresso and waited for his companion to finish chewing.

"Yes and no." The man swallowed. "Nobody knows where the cabby is. He's disappeared."

"When you say nobody, do you mean ...?"

The man nodded.

"When was his truck last seen?"

"At a gas station in Kentucky east of the cabin." The man hovered his hand over a pastry. "Can I have another one?"

"Help yourself." Viktor pushed the plate closer to the man. "We need to find out who his friends are. Where his family lives."

"I'm on it."

"Good." Viktor's phone vibrated against his chest. Business. "I must go. Feel free to enjoy your éclair. I will contact you later." He motioned to their waitress and gave her crisp new bills.

"Sir, that's too much." She gave him a broad smile.

"You deserve it, child." Viktor patted her hand. "Take care of my friend here."

Outside the café, a quaint little park sat one block away. Viktor chose a bench offering the best view of the grounds and all the approaches. He didn't get where he was by being careless.

He dialed the number. "I received your message."

"Is this a secure line?"

"Of course. And on your end?"

"Yes." The caller hesitated. "I have a job for you."

Viktor remained silent. Was he up for another job so soon? This last mess still needed to be sorted out. He'd been thinking about retiring. Maybe this would be the perfect time.

16

____

Zoe had a hard time concentrating on what Rafe was saying. Her uncle's voice echoed in her head.

"What do you think, Zoe?"

At the mention of her name, she blinked. "I'm sorry. What?"

"Are you sure you're okay?" Peter said. "You took quite a hit yesterday."

"I'm fine. Just—" Zoe pulled her phone from her pocket. With her sharp intake of breath both men rose from their chairs.

"What is it?"

"Your mom again?"

"Some monster shot my fox." She brandished her phone at them. "I need a car. Please, Rafe. I need to get to my house. She needs me."

"Fine, Zoe, but you're in no state to go out there alone." Rafe returned to his seat. "Eric is with Madison grocery-shopping, and I'm waiting for an important call from an FBI buddy."

"What about Peter?" Zoe said. "Give him a ballcap and a Rafe Private Investigations jacket for disguise. He can drive."

"I'm not crazy about the idea, but okay."

PETER FOLLOWED ZOE'S DIRECTIONS. After passing through the gate and around the curve, the cabin came into sight. He couldn't believe his eyes. It was right out of his dreams. He pulled to a stop close to the steps. Zoe's urgent voice broke his thoughts.

"Peter, I need your help."

She kneeled on the ground about three feet from a magnificent gray fox. Teeth bared, he crouched over his sibling guarding her from any interference.

"I need you to get control of the male so I can help her."

And just how did she propose he do that?

"Give me a minute."

"We don't have a minute." Zoe's voice broke. "She's dying."

"Okay." Peter scooted out of the SUV on the passenger side and removed his jacket. After all, he was a big man. Trained by the Army. All he had to do was subdue a mouth full of sharp teeth bent on protecting the sister he loved. No problem. He came around the truck to approach the fox from behind.

So much for stealth. The fox positioned himself toward the greatest threat—Peter. They rushed each other at the same time. Peter caught the animal in his jacket and held on. It was like wrestling a buzz saw.

"Here's a cage." Zoe dragged a large dog travel kennel from under the porch. "Try to get him in there while I work on her."

Sorry, buddy. He maneuvered the fox's head, still inside the jacket, through the opening. After much effort and loss of blood —Peter's blood, he left the animal to take out it's frustration on the jacket inside the box. He crossed to where Zoe bent over the prone female.

"I've managed to stop her bleeding." Zoe glanced at him. "But I can't get the arrow out of her back."

"Let me break off the tip, and we can pull it through." Peter got two pair of pliers from the car. "Hold her head. I'll do this with as little movement to the arrow as possible, but it will still hurt."

Both Zoe and the fox whimpered when the arrowhead snapped off the shaft.

Peter carefully withdrew the arrow and Zoe bandaged her side. He stood and stretched. Another arrow caught his attention. This one stuck a note to the doorframe. He walked over, yanked the projectile from the wood and pocketed the piece of paper. But not before reading it.

The money is rightfully mine!

"I've called the vet. We need to get going." Zoe slammed the passenger door shut.

Peter tossed the arrow behind his seat and climbed in.

"How did you know the fox had been shot?"

"I have video cameras set up around the property." Zoe stared out the side window.

"You just happened to view them?"

"Yes. Right."

Peter didn't believe her, but this wasn't the time to push it. Later. After her precious fox felt better. Then he'd find out what she was keeping silent about.

And warn her that silence can be deadly.

17

Viktor disliked working in a small town. People noticed strangers—especially handsome ones. Lucky for him, a large city was nearby where he could stay. It meant a commute every day in order to study his subject, but better than having to stay at some local bed and breakfast. What was all the fascination with getting to know people you would never see again?

This assignment proved harder than he thought. Her house seemed to be heavily secured. Besides, he saw no sign she'd been there recently. His client said he'd tried hiring a local who'd only succeeded in wrecking her car. Could she have realized and be in hiding?

Maybe he could work with her car. Viktor punched in a number on his phone.

WHEN ZOE ENTERED the rental house, she strode over to Rafe. "Thanks for letting us go, boss." She wanted to hug him. "The vet said we got there just in time. My fox is going to be okay."

Rafe eyed the scratches on Peter's hands and neck. "Where's my jacket?"

Zoe and Peter exchanged a glance.

"You made a noble sacrifice," Zoe said. "Trust me, Peter would be in far worse shape if it hadn't been for your jacket."

Rafe grunted. "Can we at least get some work done now?"

"You bet." Zoe picked up a box and followed Rafe across the lawn.

JUST AFTER LUNCH, Zoe's phone vibrated against her hip. A text message.

"Where's the police impound lot?" Zoe pocketed her cellphone. "They want me to check something on my car."

"Now?" Rafe descended the ladder.

She nodded. "Can you go with me?"

"We're almost finished. The last camera on Aunt Sarah's house, and then we can make sure it's all working." Rafe wiped his hands on a rag. "Can't you handle it yourself?"

"Something about this doesn't feel right." When her left ear itched, something bad happened, and it itched like crazy.

"All right. We can finish later."

"Let me ride along." Peter stepped in front of Rafe. "I promise not to get out of the car."

"Not a good idea."

"Come on, man. I helped Zoe with the foxes and nothing happened."

"You sit in the back." Rafe poked him in the chest. "And keep your head down."

"You got it."

Zoe scratched her ear.

They piled into one of Rafe's black SUVs and headed for town.

"There's something about your accident that you're not telling me." Rafe cut his eyes at Zoe.

She hated keeping things from her boss, but she liked it here. And she liked her job. He might treat her differently if he knew. Besides, the accident may have been just that—an accident. Best keep her suspicions to herself for now.

"No, boss." She shook her head. "Unless there's something weird about the guy who hit me."

"We'll soon find out. There's the gate now." Rafe pulled over. "Wait till I come around to get out of the car. Peter, stay put. I mean it."

"I will. Be careful you two."

Rafe and Zoe walked to the gate.

"Nobody in the shack." Rafe leaned closer to the fence. "Strange."

IT WORKED. The woman promised to come to the impound lot, and he, Viktor Liska, would get his opportunity. He must not fail, or she may be lost to him.

He'd chosen his spot on the roof of the building across the street and arrived early. His rifle lay propped against some sandbags for support. Although the shot wasn't long, he prided himself on accuracy. He had the element of surprise going for him. He could take his time.

The black SUV pulled to a stop exactly where he predicted. A man escorted her to the gate. Boyfriend? Bodyguard? Not important. No one could protect her from the Fox.

PETER PROMISED Rafe he wouldn't get out of the car, but he could at least be a lookout. He panned the area. Where was the policeman who usually sat in the guardhouse entrance? A stab of light bounced off the window of the building next door.

Forget his promises. Peter burst from the SUV.

"Sniper."

EYE TO THE SCOPE. Breathe in. breathe out. Finger on the trigger.

Another face filled his sights.

Viktor jerked his rifle up a few centimeters as the bullet left the muzzle.

The cabby.

18

Peter sensed the disturbance in the air. The high-speed bullet passed within inches of his head. Where was the shooter? No telltale movement, but a professional knew the drill.

"Move." Rafe pushed Zoe into the car and slammed the door.

Peter dove into the backseat just as the car took off. If the shooter was a professional like Peter thought, why had he missed? And why hadn't he taken another shot at him when he had the chance? Unless ... He stared at Zoe.

"He was shooting at you," Peter said.

She sat very still.

"Peter's right." Rafe glanced at her. "What's going on?"

"When we get back. I only want to go through this once." Zoe rubbed her right forearm.

VIKTOR RACED down the stairs to his rental car. They had a head start, but how many black SUVs with license plates that began RPI could there be in such a small town? He must find out where they went.

The stoplight at Main Street turned red. Viktor slowed. They were to his right. He joined a string of cars making their way out of town. The black truck loomed four vehicles ahead. They broke free of the city, and only two cars separated him from his prey.

Then one.

Then none.

The SUV turned right, but Viktor continued straight for a short distance until he could turn around. He approached the intersection where he'd let them go and eased onto the shoulder. Brake lights shone in the distance to his left. Were they making another turn?

Studying the area, Viktor pulled onto the road. He slowed near the spot where he'd seen the red lights. A subdivision entrance on his right. A narrow empty country road to his left. Which way did they go?

Motion in his rearview mirror caught his eye. A black SUV approached fast. No time to think. Viktor crushed the accelerator to the floor. The powerful engine responded. They'd spotted him. Now he was the prey.

Trees, fields, and fences passed in a chaotic blur. Viktor screeched around a curve. The back wheels dropped off the pavement into soft dirt throwing the car off balance. He accelerated and hung on to the wheel, spewing clods of mud across the road. The maneuver cost him some time.

He glanced in his mirror. The black SUV rounded the curve. Still there, but not gaining on him. If he could get back to town, he could lose them. Out here it was too flat with nothing to block the view for miles. He needed a street headed back toward Pleasant Valley.

A stop sign. This could be it. With a glance in both directions, Viktor maneuvered a four-wheel drift to his right onto the road and hit the gas. Tires protesting at the abuse, the car shot down the road. Would they give up?

The view in his mirror gave him the answer. No. Viktor slammed his palm against the steering wheel. He slowed as signs of civilization appeared. A rise in the road momentarily hid him from his tenacious pursuers, and a shopping center parking lot appeared on his right. He swung the car into the lot and quickly found a parking place between two other silver cars.

Moments passed. Could he have lost them? He put his finger on the button to start his car. The black SUV pulled into the lot. It rumbled down the first line of parked cars. The woman had her nose pressed to glass inspecting each car they passed. They were searching for a rental car.

He could not let them catch him. Viktor watched and waited for the moment when he'd begin the chase again.

The SUV stopped two aisles over. The men and the woman emerged, guns drawn. Now was his chance.

Viktor started his car. He let a van pass and backed out behind it. He refused to glance down the aisle to where the three inspected the other car. He turned on his blinker and headed for town. Later he would go back to the spot where he'd lost them and do some investigating.

After he switched to a different rental car.

ZOE'S STOMACH felt like she'd swallowed a piece of lead.

"This isn't the car." Rafe scrubbed a hand through his hair and searched the parking lot in all directions. "We've lost him." He slapped an open palm on the roof of the car next to him.

"Hey." Zoe yanked on his arm. "Don't set off the alarm. That would be kind of hard to explain." She couldn't take anymore.

"She's right," Peter said. "Let's go."

Rafe huffed into the driver's seat and caught Zoe's eyes in the rearview mirror. "Someone tries to kill you, and when he fails, he follows us so he can finish the job."

She lowered her gaze unable to endure the hurt and distrust in Rafe's stare.

"When we get back, I need to know what's going on. Before somebody gets hurt."

She managed a simple nod. She'd kept so much hidden for so long. Would she be able to trust these people—her friends— with her innermost secrets?

They pulled into the driveway of Peter's rental house.

"Give us ten minutes," Rafe said. He and Peter headed for their front door.

* * *

ZOE TRUDGED across the lawn to Madison's house. She could take off. Buy a new car and leave Pleasant Valley. But where would she go? And what about her mother? Zoe squared her shoulders. No. Running didn't solve a thing. Time to stand and fight. She touched the tattoo on her arm.

Ten minutes later, Zoe pulled a sparkling water from Madison's refrigerator.

"We're all here." Rafe leaned against the kitchen counter, his arms crossed tightly against his chest. "What's going on?"

She took in the faces around the room—Rafe, Madison, and Peter. These were her friends. "My mother's married name was Poole, but her maiden name was Robinson. And while *we* weren't rich by any stretch of the imagination, my mom's parents, the Robinsons, had lots of money." She swallowed. "When my grandparents passed away, their fortune was divided between my mom and her brother Harry." The words soured in her mouth, and she took another drink.

"My dad died two years ago." She blinked back tears. "And my mom has been going downhill ever since."

Madison moved next to her. "I'm so sorry."

Zoe gave her a brief smile.

"When my mom's time comes, her half of my grandparent's money will revert to me—which infuriates Uncle Harry. Especially since he's gambled most of his inheritance away already. I guess I just didn't think he'd go so far as to try to kill me over it."

"Where is this Uncle Harry?" Rafe's voice cut through the air like a saber.

"Last time I saw him was two years ago at Dad's funeral. He lived in Chicago then." A muscle in her jaw twitched. "But the other night he visited Mom's senior care home. They know about him and were able to turn him away."

"Was that what your trip to your mom was all about?" Madison touched Zoe's arm.

Zoe nodded. "He also called me the day I picked up my things at my cabin. And I'm certain he's the one who shot my fox."

"That explains this note." Peter pulled a paper from his pocket. "It was stuck to Zoe's post with another arrow."

"Of course, you saved the arrow intact." Rafe grinned at his friend.

"Wait a minute." Zoe advanced on Peter. "I never saw any note. Why didn't you mention this before?" This was exactly why she avoided getting involved with a man. Let him put a toe over the threshold, and pretty soon he was stomping around with his size twelves all over her privacy.

"You were busy helping your fox, and then ... I simply forgot with all the other stuff happening." Peter handed her the note. "I'm sorry, Zoe."

She snatched the paper out of his hand. They stood inches apart, and she peered into Peter's face. Gray eyes radiated regret and something else she couldn't quite read. Compassion? Sympathy? Pity?

He raised a hand to her cheek and wiped away the tears. She was crying and hadn't realized it until now. Silly. She backed away and grabbed a napkin.

"Must have something in my eye." She turned her back on him.

"Okay." Rafe pushed away from the counter. "First, we locate Harry.

"No." She swirled to face him. "This is my battle to fight. I'm quitting."

"Quitting? Ridiculous," Rafe said. "You need our help. What will you live on?"

Zoe straightened. "I did fine before I met you, and my mother's money is in a trust with me as trustee." She relaxed and looked at each of them. "If anything happened to any of you because of me ..."

"Now you know how I feel," Peter said.

She gazed at him. Peter. She would miss him most of all.

"I'll be in touch." Zoe walked out the front door.

Outside, Zoe sobbed on the front porch. What had she done? Sadness and grief sat like a yoke on her shoulders. How could she get through each day without the friends who had become so important to her? She didn't even own a car.

"You don't have to do this."

She turned. Peter stood so close. An arc of electricity passed from him to her—like lightening from cloud to cloud. Did he feel it too?

"Let me help you." He lifted her chin with his finger.

His touch was almost more than she could bear.

"Somewhere in the Good Book it says two are better than one." He pulled her close. "If one falls, the other can pick her up."

As she relaxed into his arms, she whispered, "Ecclesiastes four."

"Hmm."

His deep throated answer rumbled against her, and she allowed a glimmer of hope to push back the darkness. Maybe it was time to stop facing her demons alone. It would mean accepting help. Trusting people. A big step for her. Could she do it?

She pulled back and stared into Peter's strong face.

"I always thought my friends were part of the armor and protection God sent my way." Peter tucked stray curls behind her ear. "You have some remarkable friends in there, Zoe, and they're ready to help you too."

His words struck a chord deep in her spirit. But she needed time to think. Time to pray.

"Will you take me home?" She withdrew from the warmth of his arms into the chill of isolation. "I ... I just need to go home."

The pain in his eyes cut her heart to shreds. She turned away.

"I'll get the keys from Rafe."

They drove in silence. When they reached the cabin, Zoe opened her door before the car came to a full stop. She couldn't hold back her tears much longer.

But Peter caught her as she bound up the stairs and pulled her into his arms. "No matter what you decide, Zoe Poole, know this. I will always be here for you." He pressed his lips against hers in a kiss filled with strength and promise.

And then he was in the car. Gone. Honoring her wishes for time to think things through.

So, why did she feel like she'd been abandoned?

19

Viktor drove the country roads outside Pleasant Valley in his dark green sedan. When he came to the subdivision where he'd lost sight of the black truck, he slowed. Would they have been so careless as to have led him to where they lived? Or another trap?

He accelerated past the entrance and pulled over once he was out of sight. Pretending to consult a map, he surveyed his surroundings. No one and no buildings in view. Grabbing his binoculars, he entered the woods next to the plot of homes.

Viktor spied the man leaning against a tree in time to duck. He held a high-powered rifle. Why would this subdivision need a guard? Unless …

Viktor eased out of the woods. He would return at night with the proper equipment.

As he drove back to his hotel, he punched buttons on his phone and put it on speaker.

"I have found him," Viktor said. "I want you and two of your most trusted men to meet me at my hotel."

"I'll call you with an estimated time of arrival."

"Good and bring all the hardware needed."

Finally, his luck had turned.

And to think he almost didn't take the job to kill the woman. Then he would not have found Peter Grace before the others.

———

VIKTOR'S MEN had arrived with everything he needed an hour after dark. He pulled on the black turtleneck, smoothed a hand over his hair, and touched his earpiece. "Are you ready?"

"Ready when you are, boss."

Once inside the car, Viktor instructed the driver how to get to the woods he'd visited earlier. But this time, they would come from the other direction to avoid the entrance to the subdivision. If there was a guard in the woods, then one was posted at the entrance. And that guard would see their headlights.

Viktor had the driver pull off at the same place as before. They sat for a few minutes to observe their surroundings. Viktor yanked his ski mask over his head. He adjusted the strap of his night goggles, put his knife in his boot, and slipped his pistol in his back waistband. His gloves were last.

Switching to night vision, he paused to accustom himself to a world of green. He opened the car door and merged into the darkness. An animal path provided passage through the trees.

Slow and cautious steps. No broken sticks or startled birds. A green silhouette against the sky in the same place as earlier. The guard. A rifle. Goggles pushed up on his head.

Scan the houses beyond. No cars. Stay low and keep left. A break in the trees with a view to the lake. Switch to magnification.

And then he spied it. The big black truck with the RPI license plate.

He'd found them. Now he would watch and wait.

20

Madison handed Rafe a cup of coffee. "It's not the same without Zoe. Can't you do something?"

"I tried calling." He rolled his shoulders and grimaced. "No answer."

Dark circles rimmed Rafe's eyes. He missed her too, but he'd never admit it.

"Maybe we need to go out there and insist she come back." She put a bowl of scrambled eggs on the table.

"We can't get in." Peter grabbed a plate and sat down. "Her house is like a fortress."

"There has to be something we can do." The sight of Zoe's sparkling waters in the refrigerator brought tears to Madison's eyes. She swiped a hand over her cheek.

"Hi guys." Nate kissed Madison on her head and scooted a chair out from the table.

"You have time for breakfast?" she said. "I'll make some bacon."

"Only coffee for me, sweetheart."

Rafe leaned forward. "Have you found the slug from the shooting at the impound lot?"

"Not yet. But we'll keep at it." Nate smiled at Madison as she handed him a steaming cup. "We found where the shooter was, but he didn't leave anything behind."

"I'd be surprised if he had," Peter said.

Moments passed. The only sounds were swallowing and forks clanging on plates.

"Rafe." Nate cleared his throat. "I trust you to tell me if you have knowledge of a crime committed in my jurisdiction. I hope I haven't misplaced my trust."

Madison almost choked on her water. Where had that come from? She glanced between the two men.

"You haven't." Rafe faced Nate with a steady gaze.

"Is there more to this shooting I should know about?"

"If I knew anything, I'd tell you."

"Okay." Nate rose. "Duty calls. See you later."

Madison walked with her husband to his car. "Is something wrong?"

"No." He squinted against the morning sun and pulled his sunglasses out of his pocket. "It's always good to draw the line in the sand every once in a while. To make sure we both know where it is."

"I'm sure of where *I* stand." She wrapped her arms around him. "With you."

"Good. Because you're stuck with me." He nuzzled her neck. "For life." He pulled away and got in his car. "Talk to you later."

Madison waved him out of sight. Why did she feel like she'd missed something? She closed her eyes and uttered a quiet prayer.

She entered the kitchen, and Rafe studied her. In the past two years, he'd become more like a brother to her than a boss, and she could read the question in his eyes.

"Everything's fine." She patted his shoulder as she passed him on the way to the sink. "What's on the agenda today?"

"I need you to examine the arrows from Zoe's house. See if you can lift any prints or get enough skin cells for DNA."

"Too bad Zoe took the note," Peter said.

Rafe put his phone to his ear. "Rafe's Private Investigations." The corners of his mouth lifted in a smile. "No problem. We'll take care of it. Thanks for calling." He lifted his gaze to Peter. "The vet's office. The foxes are ready to go home."

"Why'd they call here?"

"They couldn't get an answer at Zoe's number, and she'd left mine as a backup."

"I guess I better go deliver them to her." Peter rose.

"Tell her—" Rafe said. "Tell her we need her."

Madison blinked back tears. "Yes. Please do."

———

PETER PULLED up to the gate onto Zoe's property and got out. He leaned in the open driver's side window and pressed hard on the horn. One, two, three, four, five. Wait five. Press five. Wait five.

The distinctive sound of a four-stroke engine sounded on the dirt road leading to Zoe's house. An ATV rounded the curve and stopped three feet from the gate on the other side. Zoe removed her helmet and her mane of sable-colored hair cascaded down her shoulders. Peter caught his breath.

"What are you doing here?" She dismounted and placed her helmet on the seat. "And why are you making such a racket?"

"You aren't answering your phone."

"Maybe I don't want to talk to anyone."

"Not even the vet?"

She advanced several steps closer. "What are you talking about?"

"I have your foxes in the back of my car. The vet's office ended up calling Rafe when they couldn't get you."

She whipped her phone from her pocket and turned it on. A single tear ran down her cheek. She swiped it away. "Thank you."

"Are you going to let me bring them up to the house?"

She cast a glance at her ATV and back at Peter.

"Come on, Zoe. We're friends, remember?"

No way the cages would fit on her ATV. She could choose to let the foxes out right here. They could find their own way back to the house, but he was hoping she'd rather have them close right away.

She opened the gate, climbed on her machine, and put on her helmet. "Don't let them out of the cages until I say."

Now to convince her to come back.

She met him in the yard. "I want to get them some grapes. Unload the cages, but don't open them." She paused at her door. "Please."

He threw her a salute and lifted the first cage from the back of his SUV. "I'm counting on you guys to help me here. Soften your mistress up so I can talk her into coming back to RPI." He set the second cage next to the first.

Zoe alit on the bottom step, a bag of grapes in her lap. "Open the cage for the male first."

Peter positioned himself behind the cage, leaned over, and undid the latch. The fox shot out of the opening and ran for the safety of the space beneath the porch. Zoe sighed.

At a nod from Zoe, Peter repeated his motions with the cage for the female. She stepped cautiously halfway out and sniffed the air. She approached Zoe and took the grape from her fingers.

And then something amazing happened. The vixen took another grape and curled into a ball at Zoe's feet. Peter stilled as Zoe stretched trembling fingers toward the beautiful animal and stroked her back.

From under the porch, the male lunged toward them snarling. The vixen growled at him, teeth bared. He backed up and sat on his haunches.

"Sorry, buddy," Peter whispered. "It can be tough dealing with an independent female."

After a few minutes, the vixen stretched and trotted under the porch. The male followed her into the shadows.

"Did you see that?" Zoe grabbed Peter and threw her head back, pure joy lit her face. "They've never let me so close."

His arms ached to hold her, but he sensed, like her foxes, he must go slow.

"She knows you saved her," Peter said. "She trusts you."

Zoe stepped away from him, but Peter caught her hand.

"Rafe said to tell you he needs you, and Madison misses you."

She raised her beautiful face to his. "And you? How do you feel?"

What was holding him back? Why couldn't he tell her she's all he thought about, dreamed about.

"I ..."

"It's okay. I've made up my mind to come back." She gave him a gentle smile. "I'll go pack."

Peter picked up the grapes Zoe had left on the steps. He squatted next to the porch and tossed them toward the foxes. "Thanks for your help, guys."

***

"I'm so glad you changed your mind." Madison pulled Zoe into a hug. "It hasn't been the same around here without you."

"After you two are done with your Hallmark moment," Rafe scowled, "do you think maybe we can get some work done?"

"You're just jealous cause you weren't in on it." Madison wagged a finger at him.

"Yeah, yeah." Rafe consulted his notes. "Madison has some items to be analyzed from the accident." He cut his eyes to Zoe. "Do you have the note from your house?"

Zoe pulled it from her pocket and handed it to Madison.

"I'll get to work." Madison grabbed a water, the note, and left.

Secrets can become such heavy burdens to carry alone. It took a near-death experience to force Zoe to do what she should have done long ago. Now it felt as if a weight had been lifted.

"What do you want me to do, boss?" Zoe said.

"Help me finish the security cams on my aunt and uncle's house. Then we need to plan how to prevent an attack from the lake."

"And me?" Peter joined them.

"Consider yourself back in intelligence, soldier. Here's a list of things I need you to research for me. These are the sites you can use and my passwords. Have fun."

21

Peter rubbed his eyes and blinked. After four hours of staring at the computer screen, he needed a break. Grabbing a ham and cheese sandwich from a deli plate left over from lunch, he headed for the back deck.

The breeze had died, and the late afternoon sun turned the water into liquid silver. He'd held his dream of a cabin for so long, and this place touched his heart in much the same way. Maybe this was where he belonged? But what about Grandma?

He picked up his phone. Needed to check on her.

"Hi Aunt Gwen. Is Grandma there?"

"She's on the patio. Let me get her."

"Peter? Is everything okay?"

The sound of his grandma's voice brought a smile to his face. Maybe he should bring her here with him. No. Bad idea. Too dangerous. Besides, she didn't want to go to her sister's. No way he'd convince her to come this distance.

"Sister almost didn't answer the phone. Did you change your number?"

"Yes, Gran." He shook his head. "Remember, I gave you a new cell phone too. I've been trying to call you, but you haven't answered."

"Oh, dear. I think I left it in St. Louis. But I have my old one."

"Please don't—"

"In fact, my neighbor called me day before last to tell me I have a package. I gave her the address here, and she's sending it on."

Peter slid down the outside of the house to sit on the deck. The sky grew dim as the sun set beyond the trees. And the air took on a distinctive chill.

"Peter, are you still there?"

"Yes, Gran. Promise me you won't make any more calls on your old phone. I'm coming to Bonne Terre to give you a new one." *Lord, please let me be in time.*

"All right, but I really don't see what all the fuss is about phones."

"I know you don't. Trust me on this, okay?" He got to his feet. "And tell Aunt Gwen not to let any strangers into the house. Oh, and call the police if anything weird happens. Got it?"

"You're scaring me, grandson."

"Good." Peter sighed. "I'm trying to keep you safe. I'll be there as soon as I can."

He peered through the sliding door to where Rafe worked at his laptop. Would he understand the urgency? No matter. Peter was going with or without his friend's help.

He opened the door. "Gran's in trouble. I'm leaving for Missouri." Peter braced for impact.

Rafe leaned back in his chair, brow furrowed. "I can't go, but I'll send Eric with you. He's my best man." He closed his computer. "You'll take the SUV. We'll get it gassed and ready. You need a gun?"

"No. I have mine." Tension flowed from his body, and he flashed a smile at Rafe. "I thought you might insist I stay, and then we'd have to fight."

"No way." Rafe pushed to his feet. "We're family now. We

take care of each other."

"Whose family needs taking care of now?" Zoe strode in through the open glass door off the deck. "Can I come?"

Peter opened his mouth to protest.

"Why not?" Rafe said. "We need some peace and quiet around here for a while. I can get both my targets out of town at the same time."

THE DOOR to his great aunt's house flew open before Peter emerged from the car.

"I'm so glad you're here. Your granny's in the hospital. We need to go." She yanked open the passenger door and stumbled backwards. "Oh, dear."

"Auntie Gwen, these are my friends, Zoe and Eric." Peter ushered her into the back seat and climbed in next to her. "Eric, make a left at the four-way."

Peter slowed his breathing. *She's hurt, but alive.*

"Tell me what happened." He took the old woman's hand.

"The package arrived." She clung to him. "You know, the one she told you about."

He nodded.

"And Kate went immediately to church."

"Church?" *What was she up to?*

"Yes." His great aunt squeezed his hand hard. "But she no sooner got back than two men pushed their way in and grabbed her." She sobbed as if her heart was breaking. "They took her, and I couldn't stop them, Peter."

"It's okay, Auntie. I'm just glad you weren't hurt as well." He put a finger under her chin and gently raised her dispirited eyes to his. "Now tell me what happened."

"About a half hour later, the hospital called. Just before you showed up."

"It's going to be okay." He patted her hand. "She's a tough old gal."

He caught Zoe's eye. Peter had walked into a trap with his grandmother as bait—but what else could he do?

"We're here." Eric pulled the large vehicle up to the main hospital door. "You go in and I'll park."

"Watch for bogeys."

"Always."

Peter and Zoe hustled his great aunt into the building and requested his grandmother's room number.

In the hall outside her door, Zoe touched his arm. "His promises are for your grandmother too."

He nodded. But the ache in his chest remained. Three years ago, Lawrence Merton bought his silence by threatening his grandparents' lives. He rearranged his entire life, gave up his dreams, but his family stayed safe. What good did that do?

Like a bad dream, Merton appeared again. Only this time, he couldn't negotiate his silence for his grandmother's life. He should have come forward back then. Speaking up may have been dangerous, but silence could be deadly too.

Peter steeled himself for what he would see beyond the door to Gran's room. A frail old woman beaten and broken. Auntie Gwen pushed past him.

"Oh, sis."

"I wondered when you would get here." Granny's voice rang out loud and clear.

Peter rushed in, Zoe right behind him.

"Grandson." She held up her right arm. "Come here. We need to talk." Her eyes widened at the sight of Zoe. "And who's this?"

"This is Zoe, a friend. Eric should be along soon. Another friend." He pulled a chair next to her bedside. Left eye black and blue. Left arm in a cast. What other injuries weren't visible? "What happened?

"You were right. I never should have used my phone." A tear

escaped her eye. "I'm such an old fool."

"But you're my old fool, and I love you." Peter's heart swelled until he thought it would break through his rib cage. "We all mess up."

"They found me." She gazed at her sister. "I'm just glad they didn't take Gwen as well. I would never have forgiven myself."

"What did they want?"

"They wanted to know where you were. I kept telling them I had no idea." She touched his cheek. "I guess they finally believed me because they blindfolded me and drove me here. They dumped me out on the sidewalk and zoomed off."

Auntie gasped. "Praise God."

Peter flashed a look at Zoe. *Yes. Praise God.*

"Peter, one more thing. I gave the package to Pastor Don for safe keeping." His grandmother patted his hand. "You need to get it from him right away."

He'd forgotten about the package.

"Did you see who it's from?"

She frowned. "L. Morton? Or something like that."

Peter froze. Lawrence Merton.

The door swung open. "Company's coming. We need to move."

Peter exchanged a glance with Zoe. She nodded. She would stay in the room with his Gran and Auntie Gwen. He squeezed her arm and left with Eric.

In the hall, the men paused, backs to the wall.

"Where?" Peter scanned the area.

"Covering all the entrances as far as I can tell."

"How many?"

"I counted five. It's a small hospital." Eric led the way around the corner. "Could be more in the parking lot."

"Where did you park?" Peter edged to a window.

"Third row from the main door. Still a lot of open ground to cross."

"I think we need some camouflage." Peter spied a door marked Hospital Personnel Only. "Let's go."

A nurse exited, fixated on her phone conversation and turned away from Peter. He grabbed the door before it closed. No one else inside. They slipped through the doorway. After a few moments, Peter and Eric reentered the hospital corridor wearing white coats with stethoscopes jutting from the pockets. Just two worn-out doctors heading home.

"It may not fool them for long, but hopefully long enough for us to get to the car." Peter took a deep breath. "You ready?"

"Let's do it."

They pushed through the glass doors and walked toward the parking lot, heads down and hands stuffed in the pockets of their white coats.

Two feet from the first row of cars, Eric fell to the ground before the sound of the shot reached their ears. A red stain blossomed on the right shoulder of his white lab coat. He rolled to the shelter of a vehicle and braced himself against the tire.

"Run." Eric grimaced and cocked his gun. "I'll cover for you."

"No." Peter crouched beside him. "Army doesn't leave men behind. How bad is it?"

"I've had worse. Where's the shooter?"

A shot zinged past Peter's head, embedding into the car door across from them.

"I'd say to our right. But we can't stay here. More are coming." Peter eyed Eric's pale face. "Can you walk?"

He nodded. "The car's two rows over and to the left."

They rose, weapons drawn, and sprinted from their cover toward the car. Eric beeped the SUV open. Bullets cut the air around them. Car windows exploded, showering them with glass. The black bulk loomed ahead.

A man stepped out from behind a van, an automatic rifle aimed at their chests. An evil grin spread across his face.

Peter raised his arm to shoot but knew his reaction time was too slow.

The grin turned to grimace as the shooter tucked the rifle under his arm and took off in the opposite direction.

Peter and Eric spun around to face their rescuer.

A man dressed in black stood three feet away. "Viktor Liska wants to talk to you."

"I'm not in a talking mood." Peter grabbed Eric and ran for the car.

Two men stepped out of the shadows and raised their guns.

"Go ahead. Shoot me, but I don't think your boss would like it."

"How about we just shoot your friend?"

"Let them go," the man in black said. "The boss said no violence."

Peter and Eric edged closer to their car.

"Mr. Liska will be around when you're ready."

"You expect me to trust a man who kills for a living?" Peter motioned Eric to get in the car.

"If he'd wanted you dead, you wouldn't be here today. What more do you need?"

"A lot. Like why'd you beat up my grandmother?" Peter jumped into the driver's seat and gunned the engine.

The man in black yelled a reply.

Peter braked and rolled down his window. The man was gone. He glanced at Eric, but it was clear pain consumed him. Had he heard the man right? The words resonated in his brain.

"We didn't do that."

If the Fox didn't lure him here by going after his granny, then who did?

22

"Eric, what happened?" Zoe rushed to the big man and helped him to a chair. "Where's Peter? Is he okay?"

He held up a hand as he caught his breath. "Peter's outside talking to the police."

Zoe couldn't think straight. Peter's grandmother and great aunt sobbed behind her. Through eyes flooded with tears, she caught sight of her tattoo. His promises of strength and protection were meant for her—and for Peter.

"Peter is safe." She gave them a reassuring smile anchored in hope. "Stay here, Auntie Gwen. I'll call my boss and arrange some protection for you and your sister."

"Thank you, dear."

"Here's the new phone for Granny." Zoe pulled a cell phone from her purse. "Please, be careful."

"You too." Tears coursed down the old woman's cheeks.

"Zoe." Eric hovered in the doorway checking the hall. "I need to get my shoulder taken care of. I'll meet you downstairs."

"HOW'S YOUR SHOULDER?" Peter glanced in the rearview mirror at Eric.

"Not bad. They wanted me to stay overnight, but ..."

"You should have." Zoe turned in her seat to glare at him. "Your injury's more than just a flesh wound."

"When we get home, I'll take care of it. I'm just going to rest here a while. Let me know when we get to the church."

"Church?" Zoe glared at Peter. "Explain to me why we're making this poor man suffer any longer than he has too?"

"The package is at the church." Peter stared straight ahead.

"This better be one important package." She leaned her head back and closed her eyes.

A mixture of emotions fermented inside her. Frustration, anger, relief ... Attraction. She stiffened. She couldn't afford romance right now. Besides, Peter came with loads of baggage.

But then, she had stuff of her own. She brushed her fingers across her lips. And his kiss still filled her dreams.

"We're here." Peter steered the big car into a parking space around the side of the building. "Eric, stay in the car. Zoe and I will talk to the pastor."

She exited with him. "What's in this bundle anyway?"

"I'm not sure, but it's from Lawrence Merton, the guy who was assassinated in St. Louis."

She stopped. "Your ex-friend? But how did he know your grandmother's address?"

"He had her name and knew the city she lived in. She's listed in the phone book." He grabbed her arm and pulled her forward. "The sooner we pick it up, the sooner we can be on the road."

"Hey." She yanked her arm away. "I don't like being shoved around, mister. We're working together, remember?"

The look he gave her made her feel a little funny inside.

"I'm sorry, Zoe." He stepped closer and smoothed a lock of hair behind her ear. "When this is all over ..."

He was way too close. She could feel his breath on her lips.

"Don't let it happen again." She gulped and stepped back. "Let's get this over with."

Attraction slid back on the list.

PETER USED his pocketknife to open the box addressed to his grandmother.

"Pastor Don was nice." Zoe pulled out of the church parking lot.

"Uh-huh."

What could Merton have sent him that would fill so much space? He'd know soon enough. Lifting the flaps, Peter stared at a mound of cotton balls with an envelope laying on top.

He slit the envelope and extracted one sheet of paper.

Peter,

If you are reading this, I'm dead. I left instructions that upon my death, this box should be sent to your grandmother whom I trust will pass it on to you.

Among the cotton you will find a thumb drive with everything on it you need. Do what I failed to do. Expose the government fraud that has been draining our country's finances for so many years.

Or you can choose to do nothing. It's up to you.
I know you will make the right decision.
I always treasured your friendship and am truly sorry for the past.

Lawrence

He sensed Zoe's curious stare.

"Well?" she said. "Was it worth the trouble?"

"Not sure. I need a computer."

"I hope you're not suggesting we try to find one now."

Her tone left no doubt how she felt about the idea.

"No." Peter dug around in the cotton balls. "We need to get back."

He extracted a black rectangular case about the size of a deck of cards. Inside, nestled in a cushion of foam, lay a thumb drive.

"What's that?" Zoe glanced over at him.

"This is dynamite. It's the reason I left the Army and ended up driving a cab in St. Louis. It's what got Lawrence Merton killed. And it's why someone wants me dead now."

"Good grief," Zoe whispered.

"Did I see you take a tin of mints out of your pocket earlier?"

"Yes." Zoe raised an eyebrow. "Kind of a weird time to need a breath mint."

"I don't need a mint. I want the tin. Can I have it?"

"Sure." She tossed the container to him without taking her eyes off the road.

"Thanks." He dumped the mints in the console.

"Hey," Zoe said. "I need those."

Using his pocketknife, Peter trimmed the foam to fit the mint tin. After snugging the flash drive into the foam, he snapped the container shut.

"Perfect fit." He put the tin in his pocket. "I'll replace this when we get back."

Peter turned away from the beautiful woman sitting next to him. He'd almost said, "when we get home." Could he make Pleasant Valley his home? Small town. People really knew each other. Helped each other out. Maybe he'd work for Rafe. He already knew people. Madison. Nate. Eric. Sarah and Ed.

And Zoe. He stole a glance at her.

"Are you hungry? Because I'm starving." She scrunched her nose.

"Sure." Peter laughed. "Let me wake Eric."

When Peter turned to poke the sleeping man, he spied a car approaching at high speed.

"Zoe, get off now."

"But I didn't see any—"

"Just do it." Peter undid his seat belt and withdrew his weapon. "Eric, wake up. Bogeys."

The car careened to the right down the exit ramp off the highway. Eric raised his head as a bullet shattered the back window.

"These windows are supposed to be bullet proof. All the bosses' cars are built the same." Eric ducked below the back seat.

"Depends on what they're shooting at us," Peter said. "What kind of fire power do you carry?"

"There's an AK-47 and an M-80 in the back. But I can't get to them unless we stop."

"Zoe, pull into the service station garage."

She yanked the wheel to the left and gunned the big vehicle into the empty service stall. Peter jumped out and pushed the button to close the door.

"Hey. What are you guys doing?" A man entered the garage through a door on the left.

"Hide. Now." Peter pointed his handgun at the man, who ran.

Eric opened the liftgate and flung bags onto the concrete floor. "Here." He cradled the M-80 in his arms and handed Peter the AK-47.

"What about me?" Zoe grabbed Peter by the arm. "I can shoot one of those too."

Peter slung the rifle over his shoulder and reached for her. Her eyes flashed with determination and strength. He wanted her to hide, to stay safe, to be a million miles away from here. But that was not who she was. She was a fighter, and if he denied her that, she would never forgive him.

"Take this." He handed her the AK-47. "I'll see what else I can find."

"Here they come." Eric peered through a row of windows in the garage door.

A car squealed into the gas station. Four men poured out of the car.

"One high powered rifle, three handguns." Eric held up four fingers. "Two in front and rifle plus one going around back."

"Where's their car parked?"

"By the pumps."

"I got a plan," Peter said.

23

Zoe gunned the motor on the big car. She felt a hesitation as the rear end smashed into the garage door, and for a second, she feared the door would hold. But the powerful engine in the SUV proved too strong a force for it to withstand. Pieces of metal and glass exploded into the gas station parking lot.

Once through, she slammed on the brakes and unloaded her assault weapon through the open window into the tires and trunk of the enemy's car. Shock waves from the explosion rocked the SUV, and flames shot into the air.

Good grief. Did gas tanks always erupt so violently? Or was something else in their trunk? She wiped a hand across her forehead. It came back red. Had she been shot?

Peter was supposed to be covering her. Where was he? Two men lay on the tarmac by the station. They pushed to their feet, holstered their guns, and stumbled off.

But no Peter. Or Eric. She pulled her revolver from her holster.

Shots sounded from the back of the service station. She crept around the outside, staying low. At the back corner, she chanced a glimpse around the building and yanked her head back. Peter and Eric were in a gunfight with a man behind a short wall.

But the gunfire wasn't what spooked her. Another man with his back to her inched his way along the wall toward the open window to where Peter and Eric crouched inside the garage. In his hand was a grenade.

What should she do? If she shot him, he would drop the grenade, and they might all be killed. Could she surprise him? Yell grenade? Shoot him and dive for cover?

What choice did she have?

"YOU COULD HAVE BEEN KILLED." Peter banged the steering wheel. "Lucky for you it was a smoke bomb."

"Well excuse me for trying to save your life. How was I to know it wasn't a grenade? It certainly looked like one." Zoe dabbed at her scalp wound and grimaced. "Next time I'll just wait in the car." She was having a hard time keeping her hands from shaking.

"Hey, I'm glad you didn't. If he'd smoked us, we'd be dead." Eric patted her on the shoulder. "How's your head?"

"Thanks, Eric." She inspected it in the mirror. "It's okay."

"And where'd you learn to shoot?" Peter glared at her. "You got him in the leg. He and the other guy managed to escape."

"For your information, I was aiming for his leg." She clenched her fists. "Just because I like to wear camo doesn't mean I'm some kind of ... crazed, bloodthirsty killer."

"You've never shot anyone before." Peter's tone changed. "Zoe, I'm sorry. I didn't realize."

"Drop it, Peter." She knew how to deal with his anger, but not his pity.

He was right, of course. The only men she'd shot glowered at her from paper targets at the gun range. Ugly, twisted faces bent on doing evil. She thought she was ready for the real thing.

But the man she shot looked like a friend from college. He'd given her a look of surprise, so sure he was drawing his last breath. She lowered her aim to his leg, praying it would be good enough.

Peter, Eric, and Zoe rode in silence for several miles.

"Still hungry?" Peter said. "I see a place we can stop at the next exit. How about it?"

"Sure."

Zoe's phone vibrated in her pocket. She pressed *Speaker*. "Rafe, what's up?"

"Where are you?"

"In Kentucky. About an hour out," Peter said. "We're getting something to eat before coming the rest of the way in. Why?"

"Skip the food. Find someplace away from people—and cameras."

"Rafe." Peter held his phone so Zoe could hear. "We're parked in back of an abandoned gas station. No cameras. We checked. What's up?"

"The news has been full of your guy. The authorities know he killed Merton. But they're also saying you're a person of interest."

"Me?" Peter's voice filled the inside of the car.

Eric sat up. "What's going on?"

"You need to get back here," Rafe said. "Zoe, you drive. Can Eric sit up front?"

"Yeah, boss."

"Peter, I want you in the back seat out of sight. On the floorboard."

"But—"

"We'll talk when you get here."

Peter pushed *End*. Person of interest. Why? Did the police

think he had something to do with his friend's murder? None of this made sense.

"You heard the man." Zoe opened the car door. "The sooner we get back to Pleasant Valley, the sooner we know—"

Peter threw his door open. A roar of frustration climbed from the pit of his stomach and escaped through his lips. Even from beyond the grave Lawrence Merton managed to ruin his life.

Again.

24

"We're here." Zoe shifted into park and glanced over her shoulder into the backseat. Peter seemed asleep. She hoped so. He needed it.

Eric eased out of the passenger seat and walked to the front door cradling his arm.

"You made good time." Rafe took the bags from Zoe. "Wake Peter. I want to talk to him."

She opened the back door. A slight frown creased Peter's brow as if he dreamed of something bad. She had a sudden urge to run her fingers down his scar. Her hand hovered over his face. With lightning speed, he grabbed her around the wrist.

He sat up, pulling her closer. His dark gray eyes captured hers as he placed her palm on his cheek. Her heart beat a staccato rhythm in her chest.

"Someday I'll tell you how I got this," he said. "But not today."

"Sorry." She took a breath. "I didn't mean ... Rafe wants to see you."

He let go of her hand and climbed out of the SUV. The corners of his mouth quirked up. "We'll talk later."

———

"I'M HERE. So, what's this about?" Peter grabbed a cup of coffee and sat across the kitchen table with Rafe.

"It's all over the news." Rafe rotated his computer screen to face his friend. "The news has a photo of Viktor Liska, one of you, and—get this—one of the itinerary you found in your cab."

"What?" Peter scrolled through the news report. "How did they get a copy?" Had he messed up?

"The big question. Who did you send copies to?"

"One to me, one to you, and one to David Underwood."

"The senator's son?" Madison said.

"He served with me in the Army." Peter nodded. "I trust him."

"If he heard you might be involved in a murder, would he give it to the police?" Madison set a plate of turkey and cheese sandwiches on the table.

"I—I don't know."

Peter hadn't seen his friend for a long time. The man he knew then may not be the same now. What would Peter do if the situation was reversed? Peter would give David the benefit of the doubt.

And so would David. They'd served together. He trusted him like he trusted Rafe.

"No. David would try to reach me first. Unless—" Peter clenched his jaw. "Unless he had no choice."

"In any case, you need to lie low." Rafe grabbed a sandwich.

"No way. I need—" Every muscle tensed. He had family to protect.

"I have a team taking care of your grandmother and aunt."

"Thanks, but what does 'taking care of' mean?"

"We've moved them to a safe house where we can keep round-the-clock surveillance."

"Bet Granny loved those arrangements." Peter chuckled.

"She gave us some grief until she saw the place." Rafe took a drink of tea. "A luxury cabin on a stream."

"Maybe I should go there to hide."

"Sorry. We need your talents here." Rafe pointed to the plate of food. "Eat something. We have work to do."

"First *we* need to talk." Nate strode into the kitchen and pulled out a chair. "I'm listening."

Several voices sounded at once. Nate held up a hand and pointed at Peter.

"Madison told you my story." Peter faced the police captain. "I knew Lawrence Merton. I gave the assassin a ride in my cab. And I found the itinerary under my seat when I was cleaning up." He squared his shoulders. "That's my only connection."

"Why'd you leave St. Louis?"

A picture of Liska's face flashed through his mind. "I recognized the look in the man's eyes. Cold. Unfeeling." Peter sighed. "And the itinerary didn't fit with him—except one way. When I heard the next day about Lawrence, I was certain Liska killed him."

"Who do you think is putting you together with all this?" Nate flashed Madison a smile as she handed him a glass of tea.

"I wish I—Viktor Liska wants to speak with you," Peter whispered.

"What?"

"At the hospital. The guy in black." Peter rose and ran a hand over his head. "Eric heard him. Where is he?"

"He's resting," Madison said.

"Sit down." Nate tugged on Peter's arm. "What did the man in black say?"

"He said ,'Viktor Liska wants to speak to you,' and he would be around when I was ready." Peter glanced at Nate.

"Why do you think he wants to talk to you?"

"Beats me." Peter put his head in his hands. "I thought he wanted to kill me, but—" He raised his head. A crazy idea scudded around the edges of rational thought.

"But what?" Nate said.

"I don't know." Peter shook his head. He needed time to think this through.

"What next?" Rafe said. "Do you need to take Peter in for questioning? Because I don't think he's safe in public."

Madison put a hand on her husband's shoulder. Nate looked at her, and Peter saw a whole conversation take place without a word uttered.

"If you'll guarantee Peter remains here, then I don't think I need to do anything more right now."

"Will you report it?" Rafe said.

"It's Friday. I'll give you till Monday. Then we'll see." Nate scanned the faces in the room. "Keep me posted. And if you need help, call. I'll do what I can." He put an arm around his wife. "Walk me to the door."

"WILL you be home for dinner tonight?" Madison wrapped her arms around her husband.

His eyes gave her the answer before he spoke a word.

"I wish I could. Tommy's disappeared."

"Doesn't he care about his parents anymore?" She pushed away from Nate. Hot tears of anger sprang from her eyes. "Or the other people trying to help him? Like you?"

"Honey." He reached for her. "He's just a kid."

"He's old enough to know better." She jerked away and turned her back on him.

"Please, Madison, I don't want to leave like this."

"Can't someone else track down Tommy?" She spun back to face him.

Was this what marriage was supposed to be like? Why did she feel this ache inside—this desire to keep Nate close?

"Jeannie wants me because Tommy trusts me." Nate touched her hair. "But I'll get someone else to go."

"No." A wave of guilt hit Madison. What was wrong with her? "I'm sorry. I don't know why I complained." She lay her head on his shoulder. "Jeannie's a dear friend. She needs you."

"Honey. Look at me." Nate took her face in his hands. "I think this case is getting to you. Bringing back a lot of—"

"Stop." Madison pulled away. "I'm fine. I just had a moment of missing my husband. Okay?" A flash of irritation swept through her. "But I'll take a break today. Sit around and eat bonbons and let them do the work."

He grinned. "I love you, Madison."

"Love you too." She blinked to hold back the tears. Was she losing her mind?

25

"Everything okay?" Peter eyed Madison's tear-stained face. Had she been this emotional before he showed up?

She nodded. "I'll clean up and get to work downstairs."

"Why don't you take the day off?" Rafe laid his napkin on the table.

"I'm fine. I'd rather keep busy." She clipped her words.

Peter caught Rafe's eye and shrugged.

"I'm going to see what's on Lawrence's flash drive." Peter pulled it out of his pocket. "Will you set me up with a computer?"

"Yeah." Rafe drained his coffee cup. "Zoe and I need to work on defenses along the lake."

Zoe gave Madison a quick hug. "See you later."

"Thanks for letting us take over your home." Peter joined Madison at the sink.

"No problem." She threw him a brief smile.

"Nate's a good guy. You two make a great couple."

She smiled again, but there was a slight quiver to her lips.

Peter paused at the door. He hoped Madison and Nate hadn't had a disagreement over something to do with him. Had he

117

made a wise decision coming to Pleasant Valley? Or had he only succeeded in putting more innocent people's lives in danger?

Too late for regrets. Now he must find the devil who killed Merton and was trying to kill him. Once he did, everyone would be safe. Peter headed for his rental home next door.

He'd start with the thumb drive. In the large family room overlooking the lake, Peter inserted the memory stick into the computer. He clicked on the icon and then on open. Good thing Rafe had state of the art equipment.

Numbers, dates, and initials populated the screen, page after page. Peter began to see a pattern, but it would take some time to interpret it properly. He printed out the first few pages and copied the information on to another flash drive for safe keeping.

"So, this is what got you killed." Peter frowned at the sheets of paper. "What does it mean?"

Rafe and Zoe entered through the sliding doors off the deck.

"What did you find?" Rafe took off his jacket and hung it on a chair.

"A lot of what seems like payments to either people or groups, but I'll need to study it further." Peter handed the copies to Rafe.

Rafe scanned the top sheet. "There's a reason you were in military intelligence, and I was a grunt." He handed it back.

"Special Forces is a little more than a grunt." Peter snorted.

"When you two are finished having a bromance moment, may I see it?" Zoe extended a hand toward Peter.

He handed her the printed pages. She studied them for a few seconds, placed them in order, and pointed to an entry.

"I think these initials may indicate Bibi Ayesha, the only female warlord in Afghanistan."

Peter moved in closer to Zoe. "You're right." He took the papers. "The rest of these may be warlords too."

"Or Taliban tribal leaders," Zoe said. "Which would make

sense with what you told us. It's probably not as simple as that, but it's a start."

Peter felt her breath on his neck. She was almost his height. He hazarded a sideways glance. Her thick lashes and the smooth skin of her cheek were close enough to kiss. His heart rate ratcheted up a notch.

"Peter." Rafe punched him lightly on the arm. "I said what do you think of the idea?"

"Great." What idea?

"Okay. You and Zoe will work on deciphering these while I finish outside."

Him and Zoe? Working together? Alone? What was it she always said?

Good grief.

"Lawrence wasn't capable of putting together an intricate scheme by himself." Peter waved the sheaf of papers in his hand. "It covered too many years and involved too many people. There had to be somebody else behind it. Somebody higher up the food chain."

"Like someone in the government?" Madison closed the door behind her. She pulled out a chair at the table in Peter's family room. "I like what you've done with the place."

"What do you mean?" Peter surveyed the scantily furnished space.

"The last time I was in here, it was filled with computer screens with pictures of the inside of my house or my face." She grimaced. "Not a fun thing to see. I like this much better."

"Ah, yes. I understand." Peter gave her a soft smile. "Want a cup of coffee?"

"No." She shook her head. "It's not tasting good to me today."

"What's this about someone in the government?" Rafe said.

"The printing on the original sheet of paper Peter brought to us—" Madison slid it from a file folder—"is a Washington, D.C. phone number. It's a cell phone. I was hoping with your connections you might be able to find out whose."

"I'll get someone on it."

Peter watched Rafe tuck the paper into his pocket. Someone in D.C. made perfect sense. Who would have had the power and influence to direct the funds to Lawrence and then funnel them to his people in Afghanistan? How high would he have had to be? Cabinet member? Or would a senator or representative have the leverage to pull it off?

Did Liska know who hired him? If so, then he'd never get a chance to talk to the police.

"And Zoe—" Madison turned toward her friend. "The fingerprint you brought me yielded the name of a local thug. He's been arrested for B&E, burglary, and disturbing the peace. I'll give his name to Nate if you want to press charges."

"Let me think about it."

"You're quiet, Peter. What are you thinking?" Rafe leaned against the table and crossed his arms.

"It might be a good idea to talk to Viktor Liska."

"Are you nuts?"

Peter raised his eyes to Rafe's. "It may be our only chance of learning the truth. If the police find him first, he'll be dead before they can get him in."

26

———

Madison struggled with memories of an ordeal she longed to forget, and this house brought it all back. A little over two years ago, she discovered her neighbor had bugged her computer and planted cameras aimed at her house. She shivered.

She needed to go home. All this talk of death and deception didn't help. Oscar rose from his place in the sun and ran to greet her.

"Hi, sweet puppy." She bent to scratch his ears.

He licked her nose.

Madison walked with him to her screened porch. She crossed a leg under her and sat on the loveseat. Oscar hopped up beside her.

She put her arms around his neck. "I wish Nate were here."

Tears ran down her cheeks. She swiped a hand across her face. "What's wrong with me?" She grabbed her necklace and prayed.

Father, why do I always feel like crying? I need Your help.

Of course. Why hadn't she thought of that before? She rose and headed for her friend's home.

"Sarah, are you busy?" Madison's eyes welled up with tears.

"Never too busy for a friend." Sarah welcomed her in with a

hug. "And my favorite pooch." She ran a hand along Oscar's side. "Would you like a cup of coffee?"

"No." Madison wrinkled her nose. "I'm off coffee lately."

"Tea then?"

Madison nodded and swiped her eyes with the backs of her hands.

"What's got you so upset?" Sarah dipped a bag of Earl Grey in the mug of hot water. "Has my nephew done something? If he has, you can be sure I'll give him a talking to."

"Not Rafe." Madison paced around the cozy kitchen twisting her wedding ring. "Although I'm not happy he's put you and Ed in danger with this case."

"Darlin', you needn't worry about Ed and me. We can take care of ourselves."

"These aren't people you can chase away with a baseball bat and a revolver." Madison rounded on her friend. "They kill for a living."

Sarah planted her fists on her hips. "Something has you in a right state, child, and it has nothing to do with the case."

Madison collapsed onto a chair. "I think Nate's having an affair with Jeannie."

Whoa. Where did that come from? Did she really think Nate would cheat on her? The realization hit her like a punch to the stomach. She did. She couldn't hold the tears back any longer.

"I know it sounds crazy, but lately, he's never home. He's always doing something to help her with some problem with her son, Tommy."

"I'm sorry, Madison, but I find the idea of Nate having an affair very hard to believe." Sarah sat next to her. "Nate's crazy about you. He's a good man who's helping a friend—your friend too."

"What if the friendship is just a cover for what's actually going on?"

She searched Sarah's eyes for—what? Agreement? Did she

really want to believe Nate capable of such deception? The truth? Sarah had no way of knowing. What she saw instead was a look of puzzlement.

"Why are you looking at me like that?"

"Madison, dear, you've been so focused on this case." Sarah reached for her hand.

"Not you too." She jumped up. "Nate keeps saying this case has me too stressed out. But I thought—I thought I could talk to you." She walked to the door. "Come on Oscar."

The big dog turned in the doorway to look at Sarah.

"Or stay here with Sarah. I don't care anymore." Madison rushed across the lawn to her dock.

At the end of the dock, she eased down and pulled her knees into her chest. What was wrong with her? She wanted to run away, get a job as a chemist, and not get involved in anybody's life. So not like her. And how could she think Nate could love anyone but her?

Oscar nudged her side. She wrapped her arm around him.

"May I sit?" Sarah appeared on her left.

Madison nodded.

"I'm sorry, sweet girl. I—"

"I think I need to see a doctor." Madison buried her face in Oscar's fur.

"I agree—"

"So, you think I'm having a nervous break-down too?" She faced her friend. "Or a brain tumor?" Fear gripped her heart. She reached for the silver cross at her throat.

"No." Sarah gave her a gentle smile. "I think something else is going on."

"What?" Why was her friend smiling at her?

"I think you're going to have a wee one."

A baby?

"I was trying to ask if pregnancy was a possibility without getting too ..." Sarah scrunched her nose. "You know."

"A baby." Madison placed a hand on her abdomen.

"It would explain why your emotions have been on such a roller coaster ride." Sarah bumped against her. "And why you've suddenly lost your taste for coffee."

"I should take a test to be sure."

"Let's do it now."

A peace came over Madison she hadn't felt for a couple of weeks. She touched her cross. *Thank You, Father.*

MADISON SURVEYED THE KITCHEN. Perfect. The sun shone through the large window facing the lake. Two placemats and settings with cloth napkins graced the table with one of her antique pottery bowls filled with apples as a centerpiece.

She directed her attention to the eggs cooking on the stove. Almost ready.

"Just us today?" Nate came from behind and gave her a hug. "What happened to the gang?"

"I told them to get their own breakfast today." She turned and wrapped her arms around his neck. "Good morning."

She pressed her lips to his and lost herself in their kiss.

The eggs. She untangled and twisted round to face the stove.

"Hey," Nate said. "I was enjoying myself."

"You wouldn't have liked your eggs burnt to a crisp." She laughed.

"A small price to pay for a kiss like that." He kissed her neck.

"Let's eat and maybe we'll have time for another before church."

"Let me." Nate carried the plate of bacon and bowl of scrambled eggs to the table.

After a blessing, Nate spooned eggs onto both plates. "How many pieces of bacon would you like?"

"Three."

He raised his eyebrows. "Three? You usually take one, or maybe two."

Madison grinned at him. "I'm eating for two now."

Nate's fork clattered to the floor. "You mean—"

She nodded. He seemed more upset than happy. Didn't he want this child?

"Madison." Nate burst from his chair and pulled her to her feet. "We're going to be parents? I can't believe it. Oh, I love you so much."

Greasy bacon hands embraced her, and his kisses rained down on every inch of her face and neck. Her heart turned cartwheels.

She was definitely going to need to change for church.

WHAT A GREAT DAY. Breakfast with Nate. Then church and lunch out. Madison hadn't realized how much she needed a real break from life. She swiveled her head to gaze at her handsome husband and placed a hand on her belly. She let out a sigh of contentment.

"You look happy." Nate grinned at her.

"I am."

He frowned, and her body tensed. What was going on in that policeman brain of his? Whatever it was, she sensed an argument coming.

"I've been thinking," Nate said.

Never a good start.

"You need to be careful for the next seven or so months. Why don't I get Bernadette to stay with you?"

She knew it was coming. The protective mode. And she refused to go along with it.

"Nate. Pregnant women do most everything they've been doing right up until their due dates." She gave him a stern look. "I don't need a bodyguard. Besides, Bernie is a detective now. You can't just pull her away from her cases and expect her to play nursemaid."

"Then I can get somebody else." He pulled into their driveway and turned pleading eyes to her.

Her heart melted. He was so concerned about her.

"What if I ask Eric to stay with Sarah and Ed, and have Zoe come stay with us? Would you feel better?"

"Yes." Relief filled his eyes.

"And I have Oscar."

"You mean the dog who thinks with his stomach?" He laughed. "Not sure we can count on him in a fight."

He had a point. But her sweet dog knew when she needed a shoulder to cry on and a doggie kiss on the nose. And that was enough.

"One thing I have decided." Nate opened the car door for her, his face grim. "I'm going to bring Peter in for questioning."

"Why?" A spark of fear twisted her insides.

"If I do, it lessens the threat to you and Sarah and Ed."

"But what about Peter?" Madison followed her husband inside. "You're putting his life in danger. How can you justify it?"

"What am I supposed to do?" Nate ran a hand through his hair. "I'm the police captain." His eyes bore into hers. "I will do everything possible to keep him safe, but I need to talk to him on the record."

"When are you going to take him in?"

"Tomorrow morning."

Peter was her friend. But Nate was her husband and the father of her child. Madison walked to the window overlooking the lake. Her fingers caressed the cross at her throat.

"Thanks for letting me come in with you today." Peter entered Nate's office, a little nervous. Was he about to be arrested?

"I'm trying to keep this as low key as possible." Nate moved behind his desk. "I'll record it myself, and we'll have Detective Jeannie Jansen with us as witness." He pointed to the door. "Here she is."

Peter had seen photos of the blonde detective around the Zuberi house. Introductions made, Jeannie closed the blinds and pulled up a chair. Peter and Nate took seats on both sides of the desk.

"Why don't you start?" Nate said.

"First, let me say I'm not proud of how I handled what happened three years ago." Peter glanced at the recorder. "I hope you have a lot of tape in that thing. This could take a while."

After thirty-three minutes, Peter took a drink of water. "I showed up on Rafe's doorstep—well, his aunt and uncle's—looking for help. I needed help to find out who killed my friend." He shifted his gaze between Nate and Bernie. "And I think I've figured out part of the puzzle."

"What do you mean?" Nate said. "I thought it was Viktor Liska, the Fox?"

"Yes. But who hired him?" Peter leaned forward. "I think someone in the government is trying to keep a lid on what went on in Afghanistan. They had Lawrence killed, and now they're after me."

"Why you?"

"Because Merton texted me the night before he was murdered. He wanted to see me. Urgent. I ignored it." He raised his eyes to them. "I think this person is able to access phone records and thinks I know what Merton knows—knew."

"Do you?"

"Not then, but—"

A banging sounded on the door. "Captain Zuberi. We need to talk with you. Now."

Nate and Jeannie rushed to their feet.

"You stay here," Nate said. "Not a peep. Understand?"

Peter nodded.

Nate and Detective Jansen slipped through the door. Peter padded across the room and put his ear close to the blinds covering the glass.

"We're from Homeland Security," a male voice said. "And we're here to take custody of Peter Grace."

"Peter Grace?" Nate said.

"Don't act stupid, Captain Zuberi. We know he's in your office."

Peter raised a slat of the blinds just enough to see one man had his back to the window. The other was in profile. His nose had been broken at one point and never set.

"How do you know?"

"We know everything."

"Not good enough," Nate said. "Where's your warrant?"

"We don't need one."

"In my precinct you do."

Nate moved to block Peter's view.

"You want Mr. Grace, get a warrant. Good day, gentlemen."

"We'll be back."

Footsteps sounded on the tile floor.

"Do they need a warrant? Jeannie said.

"Yes," Nate said. "But something doesn't feel right."

They'd found him. Adrenaline pushed through Peter's system. He needed to get back to the lake.

Think. Plan. Execute.

MADISON WIPED her hands on a towel before answering the phone. "Nate, what's wrong?"

"Peter climbed out my window and disappeared. If he shows up back there, tell him I'm inclined to believe him about ... his theory."

"What theory?"

"We'll talk more in person. Love you."

"Love you too." *What happened at the station house?*

"Was that your husband?" Peter came up behind her.

She swirled and grabbed a butcher knife.

"Easy now." He sat at the kitchen table.

She replaced it and didn't approach him. "What happened today?"

"It was fine until two guys showed up supposedly from Homeland Security demanding to take me into custody." He tapped the table with his fingers. "But something wasn't right about them."

"Nate must agree with you. He just told me to tell you he believes your theory."

"Good." Peter sighed. "Makes things a whole lot easier."

"Are we talking about the idea of a government official behind the assassination?"

Peter nodded.

The D.C. phone number she lifted off the paper. But how

had they discovered Peter was at Pleasant Valley Police Department? Nate was so careful.

They'd all been careful.

A chill ran through her. "How did you get back to the lake?"

"I called Rafe. Why?"

"They've had time to bring in more people to search the area. Pleasant Valley's not a large city." She put a hand on her belly. "Where are Rafe and Zoe now?"

"What's wrong, Madison?"

"Nothing. I—"

The realization hit her. She wasn't risking one life but two. This wasn't just something happening *to* her. Her choices impacted a human being who couldn't decide for his or herself.

"I'm going to have a baby."

She watched as the full meaning of her words impacted her new friend. Happiness for her and Nate gave way to horror and shame.

"Madison, you need to get somewhere safe." Peter pushed to his feet. "You still have family in St. Louis, don't you?"

His desperation scared her. She managed a nod. Maybe Nate was right. She did need a bodyguard. What should she do?

"Then get out of here. Before it's too late."

"Too late for what?" Rafe's throaty voice sounded from the doorway.

28

"Madison, how cool." Zoe flung her arms around her friend's neck.

Zoe wanted kids one day. After she met and married the right man. She cast a veiled glance at Peter. Could he be the one? She shook herself. No use thinking about that now. She had a job to do—and her mother to protect.

"I don't know if leaving town is such a good idea." Zoe twisted the cap off a sparkling water. "The bad guys could decide to get rid of us. The fact is we all have access to the flash drive now. We're all liabilities." She looked around. "Safety in numbers. Right?"

"I'm not sure Nate will see it the same way," Peter said.

"I think he'll be okay as long as one of you is with me at all times." Madison covered her face with her hands. "Guys, I'm so sorry to put this on you right now."

"Hey." Rafe laid a hand on her arm. "Babies are always something to celebrate. God's got this. And so do we."

Another reason Zoe loved working at RPI. The team felt like a family. Something she'd missed growing up.

"Peter, you're confined to the rental for now. Zoe, you stay here with Madison." Rafe studied the view of Lake Pleasant. "We need to get our perimeter defenses in place."

PETER CHECKED FOR SOUND. Birds chirped and small animals scuttled around. Good. The cameras worked well. Crisp, clear pictures covered almost every angle of approach to the rental, the Zuberi's home, and Sarah and Ed's place.

Hang on. A familiar black car drove up to the rental. Nate and Jeannie got out. Peter's pulse ratcheted up a notch.

"Captain." He opened the door.

"Peter." Nate nodded at him. "May we come in?"

He stepped aside. Grim faces and stiff body language told him all he needed to know.

"We need to bring you down to the precinct again."

At least Nate looked sorry. But regret wouldn't keep him from doing his job. He was a professional—like Peter used to be. A wave of envy and regret rolled through him.

"What is it this time?"

"We found the mon—" Detective Jansen said.

Nate held up a hand. "We'll talk about it at the station. You need to let Rafe know?"

"Yeah. Just a minute."

Was Detective Jansen about to say money? But he already told Nate about the money. He balled his fists as rage filled his body. They'd done it again. Used funds placed in a bank account in his name to implicate him in a crime.

The corners of his lips lifted in a smirk. This time, they may have outsmarted themselves.

At the station house, Nate got right to it.

"We have a video of you depositing the sum of twenty-five thousand dollars in a newly opened account in Kentucky right after you arrived."

"Impossible. I didn't open an account in Kentucky," Peter said. "In fact, I don't have any checking accounts in my name any longer. I closed the one I had and put all my money into a CD before I left St. Louis."

Nate pivoted his laptop toward Peter. A picture of a man who looked almost identical sat at a desk in a bank filling out a deposit slip. The amount was clear. Twenty-five thousand.

Peter leaned in and studied the photo. "That's not me."

"Sure looks like you to me." Detective Jansen snapped the computer toward her.

"Look closer. The people setting me up didn't do their homework." Peter pointed to the man's left cheek. "No scar."

Jeannie whipped her attention to Peter. "I'll be." She shoved the computer in front of Nate. "He's right. Those idiots forgot the scar."

"Now we have a real problem." Nate ran a hand through his hair.

"Where'd you get the video?" But Peter already knew the answer.

"The guys from Homeland Security." Nate's brown eyes narrowed. "Supposedly from Homeland Security."

"They may be." Peter shrugged. "Who knows? I have no idea who's involved in this."

"What do you have that's so valuable to these people?" Jeannie said.

"It's complicated. Proof about government money funding our enemy in Afghanistan so some greedy men back home could make a profit." Peter rubbed his forehead. "The money helped them buy weapons to kill our soldiers. Who knows how many of our men were lost because those ..." Fury choked the words in his throat.

Nate made a note on his phone. "Where's the proof?"

"On a flash drive." Peter calmed. "The original is in Rafe's safe. A copy is with his techs being analyzed."

"Good." Nate rose. "Let's get you back to the house."

"What about the Homeland Security guys?"

"We'll let Jeannie deal with them." Nate grinned. "They won't know what hit them."

PETER'S DOOR swung open before he could get the key in the lock.

"You okay?" Rafe spoke to Peter but looked past him to Nate and waved.

"Fine." Peter stepped inside. "Everything's good."

"Great. What did they want this time?"

"I was right. Somebody in the government is behind this. They tried to frame me with a video, but it didn't work."

"We've found the hive," Rafe said. "Let's see what comes after us."

Peter followed Rafe to the open living room/dining room at the back of the rental. Zoe gazed up at him from peeling an orange. Strands of her sable-colored hair framed a heart-shaped face and trailed along her long neck to her broad shoulders. Traditional olive green T-shirt and camo pants today. But it was those violet eyes that made his heart skip a beat.

"How did it go?" Madison handed him a cup of coffee.

He hadn't noticed her there. "False alarm." He took a seat across from Zoe.

"We've made some decisions." Rafe propped a hip on the arm of a chair. "Since we can't stop people from using the path behind the houses, we're adding motion sensors in the yards of all three houses. Alarms will go off and at night, spotlights will go on as well."

"We'll be getting alarms for dogs and children—not to mention any deer wandering through."

"It can't be helped." Rafe stared out the glass doors onto the deck. "It's only till we catch this ... jerk."

"We're also putting sensors on each of the piers," Zoe said. "Between those and the lawns, count on a lot of false alarms."

"I, for one, won't mind a bit," Madison said.

"I'll take inventory tomorrow," Rafe said. "Eric, I may need you to go into town for some things."

"I'll go with him." Zoe straightened.

"You've got a contract on your head, remember?" Rafe made the shape of a gun with his hand and pointed it at his head. "Too dangerous. Tell Eric what to get."

"I can't." She stood. "If they don't have exactly what I tell him, he won't know what to substitute." She put her hands on her hips.

Rafe frowned at her.

She stared back.

"You wear a disguise and Eric goes with you." Rafe spun on his heal and tromped into the kitchen.

"Wait a minute." Peter's heart went to his throat. "I'd like to tag along." Zoe out there in the open—Eric or no Eric—set off all his protect-at-all-cost, neurons.

"No." Rafe growled from the next room. "Bad enough I'm letting one target out on the streets of my town. I'm not releasing two." The front door banged shut.

"I think that's my cue." Zoe slid open the back door.

"Hang on." Peter caught up with her. "I don't like the idea of you going into town."

She raised an eyebrow. "After what we went through at the hospital in Missouri and the gas station in Kentucky, now you're worried about me going to a hardware store with Eric in Pleasant Valley?"

He captured her eyes with his. "Yes. I ..." How could he tell her how he felt when he wasn't sure himself? All he knew was he liked having her in his life.

"You what?" She leaned toward him.

"Zoe, you're still here?" Madison said. "I thought you'd be home by now. Would you walk us back, Peter?"

He sighed. "Sure."

At the door, Zoe leaned over and gave him a kiss on the cheek. "Sweet dreams."

Sweet dreams indeed.

29

Peter followed his nose to the coffee pot and poured a large mug of the steaming brew before taking a seat at the table. This morning needed a heavy dose of caffeine.

"Rough night?" Rafe glanced at him above his computer screen.

Peter grunted.

"Want to talk about it?"

"Yeah, but let me drink this first." No way he'd make any sense before held his second cup.

Peter surveyed the now familiar view outside his wall of windows. The lawn was losing its coat of green, and the trees sported a mixture of colors, their leaves falling at the slightest breeze. Wouldn't be long before it was too cold to sit on the deck.

If he were around.

"What kept you up last night?" Rafe said.

Peter pulled his attention back to work. "I don't like the idea of Zoe going into town."

"Me either, but she's a big girl as you may have noticed." Rafe closed his computer.

"But you're her boss."

"Hey. You didn't like it when I tried to play nursemaid to you."

"A different thing altogether."

"How?"

"It's ..." How was it different? Because she was a woman, and he was a man? No. His shoulders slumped. "It's not. But I still don't like it."

Rafe slapped him on the back. "I get it." He punched the speaker button on his phone. "Rafe Private Investigations."

"I'd like to speak to Rafe O'Connell please."

"You got him."

"Great. David Underwood here."

Peter opened his mouth to speak. Rafe held up his hand.

"Should I know you?"

"Didn't Peter tell you about me? I'm his friend from the Army. He told *me* about *you*. I just assumed ..."

"Oh, yeah. David." Rafe put a finger to his lips. "What's up?"

"Have you seen the news? I'm really worried about him."

"Yeah. Me too."

"Listen. I don't think it's a good idea to say too much over the phones. I took the chance and came into town. Can we meet and talk about how we can help him—if anything?"

Peter and Rafe locked gazes over the table. He hadn't seen or spoken to David for years. And now here he was. Right here in Pleasant Valley. Something didn't smell right.

"Where are you staying?"

Silence.

"A little B and B off the main drag."

"Do you know where the Main Street Grill is?"

"Yes. I ate dinner there last night."

"Meet you in about an hour. I'll be sitting at a table in the window wearing an RPI jacket."

"See you then." Click.

"Did he sound like David?" Rafe said.

"Seemed to." Peter closed his eyes. Not sure. "It's been a long time."

"No matter. When I meet him, you'll be in a car nearby and can let me know if it's him." Rafe stood and shrugged into his jacket. "Or not."

PETER SLOUCHED in the backseat of the black truck. The side street across from the Main Street Grill gave a great view of the front window. A man approached the entrance from Peter's right, hat pulled low on his forehead. Peter raised his monocular but too late to see his face. The man entered and walked past Rafe to a booth nearby.

Something familiar about the guy. Not David but someone he knew. He sat with his back to the window, and when he removed his hat, he was ... bald? He lowered the monocular. Who did he know who was bald?

"Any sign of him yet?" Rafe's voice sounded in his ear.

They had agreed to use two-way communicators so Peter could let Rafe know if the man was David. And Peter could hear their conversation.

"No. Just a guy—" Peter stopped. "Hang on."

A tall, sandy-haired man strode down the sidewalk like he owned the town. David. He hadn't changed a bit.

"Here he comes."

The sounds of introductions, chairs scraping, and a waitress taking orders played out in Peter's ear as he watched from his hidey hole. He adjusted the earpiece and sat a little straighter.

"Thanks for meeting with me."

"How did you find me?" Rafe said. "I'm not on any social media. I work off word of mouth."

David gave a low chuckle. "My dad's a senator, Mr. O'Connor. I have access to all sorts of information."

"You fed my name into a bunch of databases and found out I have a PI license."

"Something to that effect."

Peter lifted the monocular to his eye. Rafe's stony face came into his field of vision. He shifted his view to the right. David lowered his drink to reveal a smug smile. Had he always been like that? Or had he changed since Peter knew him?

"In any case, I'm worried about Peter. I would have thought you would be to. Especially after opening the packets he sent to you and me."

David accessed the letter containing a copy of the itinerary. Could he have given it to the newspapers? A chill ran through Peter's body. Followed by a burning rage from the bottom of his feet that shot to the top of his head. He reached for the door handle.

As he did, Peter realized he was not alone on the side street. A man lurked in the shadow of the building, and his gaze focused on the scene playing out in the window of the Main Street Grill across the street. Peter shrunk down on the back seat of the pickup, thanking God for its highly tinted windows.

"We have company. Man in the shadows next to me. May also be a man inside. The bald guy behind you is familiar."

Peter brought the monocular to his eye just in time to see Rafe turn toward the window as if in thought.

"I see."

Peter caught the response meant for him.

"I put the packet in my safe. Unopened." Rafe glared at David. "It said in the event of his death. I haven't heard he's died yet. Have you?"

Peter swung the monocular to David—who flushed. A point in his favor.

"When I saw he was wanted for questioning in the assassination of Lawrence Merton, I decided to open it. In case it had anything in there to help him."

"And did it?"

"Just a copy of the same itinerary I'd seen in the papers. And a letter explaining how he got it." David sighed. "I don't think it's enough."

"So why come to me?"

"You're a private investigator. Can't you investigate? Find him at least? I mean, you've got guys gua—" David coughed and grabbed for his water.

"I've got guys what?" Rafe said.

"You've got guys. Lots of help."

Silence.

"Where are you staying?"

"I need to find another place. Let me call you tomorrow."

Why was David being evasive? Small town. Easy to find out where a stranger was booked. And what was he about to say? Guarding what? The entrance to the subdivision? The rental house?

His grandma and aunt?

Peter studied David through the monocular as he stood and put on his jacket. The bald man in the booth prepared to leave as well. As he turned to go, Peter focused on his face and almost dropped his spy piece. The face filling his field of vision was Viktor Liska, the Fox.

He needed to let Rafe know.

"The Fox. Behind you."

Rafe stood. Peter saw his right hand slide over the butt of his gun. But when Peter shifted his view back to the booth, the Fox had vanished.

David left. The man by the building disappeared as well.

"Did you see where he went?" Rafe's voice sounded once more in his ear.

"No. Want me to look for him?"

"No. I'm coming to you." Rafe pushed through the door of the Grill. "We'll take a ride around downtown. See if you spot him."

No luck. The man in the hat was gone. And so was David. Leaving lots of questions behind.

"What do you think?" Rafe spoke first.

"Too many questions."

"Like?"

"Is David a good or bad guy? Did he leak the itinerary to the media? If so, why?"

Rafe nodded. "And the 'guys guarding' thing was a major slip on his part. He knows more than he's telling."

"And the Fox. What was he doing there?"

"Don't forget the man in the shadows next to you. What did he look like?"

"I only got a glimpse of him. I was busy trying not to be seen myself." Peter raised a hand to his head. "He was wearing a cap. What I call a racing cap. Shaped like a wedge. Low in the front and higher in the back."

"Was he with David or Liska?

"Don't know," Peter said. "I feel like I'm back in Army Intelligence. Where do we begin?"

"We find out where your old Army buddy is staying."

30

Again, lady luck had smiled on Viktor. He followed Peter and his friend into town. When Peter remained in the car, Viktor donned a disguise and entered the restaurant after his friend in the jacket. Who was this man? His economical movements suggested a military background.

When the sandy-haired man joined Peter's friend at his table, Viktor scooted a few inches closer in order to hear their conversation. He needn't bother. The third man spoke as if no one else was around. Viktor learned much important information.

Peter's friend was Rafe O'Connor, a private investigator. He and Peter seemed to be wary of this other one, David Underwood, a senator's son, even though he claimed to be a friend of Peter. But one of the most valuable things Viktor learned was from the sound of David's voice.

This was the man who had hired him to kill Lawrence Merton.

This was the man who had double-crossed Viktor.

He would be Viktor's last target before he retired to Europe. To do this, he must talk to Peter.

And Viktor knew just how to persuade Peter to meet with him.

PETER GLANCED AT RAFE. "ANYTHING YET?"

Rafe shook his head. "You?"

"No." Peter grabbed his water bottle and took a swig. "David must have used an alias or paid someone to keep his name off the hotel records."

"I'll make some calls." Madison picked up her phone. "Maybe I can pick up on something."

Zoe came in with Eric in tow. Gone were the camo pants and top. Instead, she wore blue jeans that showed off her long legs and a collared white shirt rolled up to her elbows. Her lush sable-colored hair pinned high on her head.

Peter took a step in her direction. Her slender neck beckoned his kiss. He stopped. What was he doing?

"Do I look different?" She twirled.

"You look like a super model trying to go incognito." Madison laughed.

"How about now?" Zoe clamped a ballcap on her head.

"Sorry. You're still too amazingly beautiful." Madison hugged her. "But you don't look like the Zoe I know because she always wears camo. This should work."

"Peter, what do you think?"

"I—" He gazed at her. "I agree with Madison." Beautiful. Amazing. Perfect.

Zoe blushed and scratched her left ear.

ZOE SAT in the back seat behind the heavily tinted windows of the SUV while Eric drove them into town. She loved it here in Pleasant Valley. The lake, the surrounding farmland, the prosperous town with its quaint downtown. Cincinnati sat only an hour away for all the other things like concerts, museums, and major shopping. The best of two worlds.

Eric parallel parked in front of the Emporium. One of the perks of a small town—an old-fashioned hardware store.

From the tinkle of the bell over the door to the squeak of the wooden floors, Zoe loved it all. Including the smells. Bolts and nails. Screws and washers. Boxes and boxes of them everywhere. Rolls of wire hanging from the wall. Batteries galore. She was in her element.

As she searched through a box of nails, a balding man in a navy jacket approached Eric.

"Is that your black SUV out there?"

"Yeah," Eric said.

"Hey, man. I'm sorry. I caught it with my panel van trying to turn around." The man pointed out the window. "Would you come out so we can figure out what to do?"

Zoe glanced at Eric who raised his eyebrows at her. She nodded. She was fine. He could take care of the car. She watched him leave with the man then returned to her task.

A noise from the front. Shouting.

"I think your friend's in trouble." The clerk behind the counter rushed to the door.

Zoe dropped the nails and whirled.

Arms grabbed her from either side, dragging her backward. A large hand clamped over her mouth. If she could bite him, she'd call out for help, but the restraint was too tight. Someone dragged her out a door into the alley. Where was Eric? Had they killed him? Were they going to kill her too?

Not if she could help it.

She went limp. The hand released from her mouth. She jerked her left arm up to her face. Her teeth sunk deep into the hand of her attacker. A scream and she was free. Now for the other guy. She yanked her right arm forward. He took a step and hung on. Twist and a punch to the jaw. He fell to the bricks. A spin kick to the head of her left-hand attacker. He joined his partner.

She stopped in a crouch, ready to go another round. No movement. Time to tie them up and call the police.

"Impressive," the man said behind her.

She spun, prepared to do battle, but the man stood out of range of her long legs, and he aimed a gun at her heart.

Viktor Liska. The Fox.

"I CAN TELL by your eyes you know who I am." Viktor studied her. A beautiful woman. With skills. He *was* impressed. "I am supposed to kill you."

"Then why don't you?" Zoe straightened. "I'm not afraid to die."

"Aw, fearless." He motioned her toward a panel van nearby. "I told the man who hired me you were on vacation in Europe and gave him his money back."

"Why?"

"You would be a terrible loss for the world." He smirked. "And I need you to do something for me." He never liked killing women anyway.

"I thought so."

"I need to talk to Peter Grace. You are his girlfriend."

She shook her head. "We work together. I'm not—"

"I have seen the way he looks at you. The same way he looked at the photo of the cabin in his taxi." Viktor smiled at her. "If you are not his sweetheart, he at least wants you to be in the future." Lucky Peter. Viktor would like such a woman in his life.

"Why should I bring Peter to you?" Her body stiffened. "So you can kill him?"

"You are not listening. I do not want to kill him. I want to talk to him." Viktor clenched his teeth. "I want to get the man who double-crossed me."

The door from the hardware store opened, and the man in the navy jacket rushed through. "The ambulance is here."

"Help them to the van." Viktor indicated the two men down the alley. "We need to go."

"What about Eric?" Zoe stepped toward Viktor.

"He will be fine. A shot to make him sleep. Nothing more," Viktor said. "Get in the van."

The man in the navy jacket tied her hands.

"Tie her feet as well," Viktor said. "I have seen the damage she can do with those long legs."

PETER'S COMPUTER SCREEN DIMMED. He touched a key to bring it back into focus. If only it were that simple with his mind. Since Zoe left for town, he'd been staring at the same page from Lawrence Merton's flash drive. Numbers and initials. He scrolled down. None of it made any sense.

Hang on. A pattern. Repeating entries. Could this be the key?

"Zoe's been taken." The urgency in Rafe's voice behind him cut through his thoughts.

Peter sprang to his feet and grabbed Rafe by his shirt collar. "I told you I needed to go with her." He should have insisted. Now ...

"Calm down." Madison laid a hand on Peter's shoulder. "We need to work together if we're going to get her back."

He shrugged her hand off and released his grip. Think. Plan. Execute. First get his anger under control. Deep breaths.

"I'm sorry," Rafe said. "I thought ..."

"I know. She's a big girl." Peter waved a hand at him. "You're right. I can't be with her 24/7. What happened?"

"They got to Eric first. Knocked him out." Rafe went back to his chair. "Grabbed Zoe through the back door."

Madison placed one hand on her stomach and the other on her necklace. "What's the plan?"

"You call Nate," Rafe said. "Then, we wait for the kidnappers to get in touch."

31

Did Zoe hear right? Viktor Liska had been double-crossed? What kind of crazy person would dare do such a thing and risk getting killed? And how could Peter help him?

The man in the navy jacket helped the other two limp to the front seats of the van. He climbed into the back and sat on the floor, pressing himself into the corner as far from Zoe as possible.

"Get me her phone." Liska, who sat in one of the two seats facing the back of the van, snapped his fingers at the balding man.

He crawled over to where Zoe lay on her left side and nudged her. "Where is it?"

"My right pants pocket."

The van started to move.

A sheen of sweat covered the man's face, and his fingers shook as he reached across her body. He'd seen the damage she'd done to his friends. He pulled her phone from her pocket, and she jerked, sending him scuttling backwards like a crab.

Viktor scoffed. "What can she do? Her hands and feet are bound you fool." He yanked the phone from the man's grasp. "Now we call Peter."

"You know I work for Rafe Private Investigations, right? Peter is a close friend of Rafe." Zoe studied Viktor's expression. "You're about to wake a wild tiger."

Viktor sprang from his seat to where Zoe lay on the van floor. He grabbed her chin in his fingers. "And what do you think I am? A housecat?"

For the first time, fear swept through Zoe and she shuddered.

He released her and returned to his seat. "Much better. Now you understand who you are dealing with." Viktor swiveled to peer out the front window. "Turn here and head out of town."

"He'll know it's a trap." Zoe fought to keep the tremor from her voice.

"What is the passcode for your phone?"

She stared at Viktor. Could she hold up under torture? Was it worth it? Her mother's face swam before her eyes. But even if she cooperated, would he let her live?

"Zoe—may I call you Zoe?" Viktor sighed. "I only want to speak on the phone. Tell him why I wish to talk to him. If he agrees, we will meet." He smiled at her. "Okay?"

If she called Peter, Rafe could get a fix on her phone. He and his guys could find her.

"Okay." She held out her bound hands for her phone. "I'll make the call and hand it to you."

Viktor hesitated, then gave her the phone.

Peter's phone rang three times. Pick up. She closed her eyes. *Lord, please let him answer.*

"Zoe? Where are you?"

"I'm—" Tears choked her words.

Viktor took the phone from her fingers. "Peter. You are a hard man to find."

MOLTEN FURY RAN through Peter's veins. "What have you done to Zoe?" He jabbed a finger at Rafe who started the track on Zoe's phone.

Madison took her cell phone and walked across the room.

"Nothing, my friend. I assure you."

"I'm not your friend." Peter's voice cut the air like surgical steel. "If you hurt her, I'm your worst nightmare."

"I have no intentions of touching her. I only wanted to get your attention and the delightful young lady seemed to be the only way." Viktor's tone changed. "We need to talk."

"I'm listening." Peter watched Zoe's trace signal move across Rafe's computer screen. They were in a vehicle.

Madison returned and wrote on the notepad next to them. *Called Nate.*

"First I must ask how you knew I killed Lawrence Merton."

"You were careless. The itinerary from your briefcase fell out inside my cab."

"I had no itinerary with me. It is on my phone so I can delete it after the job is completed."

"Then where—"

"My thoughts as well," Viktor said. "Maybe planted by the zealous new doorman at the hotel?"

Peter closed his eyes and pictured the scene again. The doorman's face came into view. Nondescript except for his nose which had been broken and never set.

The man from Homeland Security.

"You are quiet. What are you thinking?"

"Nothing. Just trying to remember what he looked like."

"My private car was canceled forcing me to call for a cab."

"You could have gotten any cab."

"Yes. So why was it yours? The one man in the city who had a history with Lawrence Merton. Someone wanted you to pick me up, Peter."

Could Peter believe a man who killed for a living, a man

without a conscience? But he realized Liska stated the nagging doubt he hadn't been able put into words himself.

"I was set up," Liska said. "Maybe you as well. Unless ..."

"Unless what?"

"Unless you are part of it. In which case, you are dead."

32

Viktor spied a black SUV in the back window. Time to end the conversation. "Your friends have found us, Peter. I will be in touch." He copied Peter's number into his phone and replaced Zoe's in her pocket.

"We have company. Speed up. When we get around the next curve, slow and we will roll the girl out."

Viktor motioned to the balding man to help him. As the van slowed, he threw the sliding door open on the side and they rolled Zoe out onto the pavement.

"Now go."

Viktor watched as the SUV skidded to a halt and four men ran to Zoe lying in the middle of the road. Such a remarkable woman. He hoped she wasn't badly hurt.

PETER PROWLED around Madison's living room with an empty mug in his hand.

"She's fine," Rafe said. "Just a few scrapes and bruises."

Peter would judge for himself once he saw her.

"Let me take that." Madison pulled the cup from his grip. "They should be here any minute."

The car pulled into the driveway and Rafe helped Zoe out of the back seat. Peter walked toward her. Bandages covered her left cheek and hand. Blouse torn at the shoulder and black streaks on her jeans. He stopped in front of her.

"I'm okay." She placed her right hand on his arm. "Help me to the house. The EMTs gave me some pain meds. I'm woozy."

Eyes bright. Hand warm. A little smile lifting the corners of her mouth. She was okay. He could relax.

"I'll help you go anywhere you want," Peter said.

She rolled her eyes. "A comfy couch will do for now."

"I'm sorry, Zoe." Peter held her arm as they navigated the trip across the lawn. "I never should have come to Rafe for help."

She stopped and glared at him. "If you hadn't come here, we never would have met. Is that what you want? Because I sure don't." She removed his hand from her arm. "I think I can make it from here on my own."

"That's not what I meant." Peter caught up with her on the porch. "You know how I feel about you."

"Do I?"

The door opened. "Come in here and sit down." Madison put an arm around Zoe's waist and guided her to the couch in the family room. "Nate and Jeannie are on their way."

Madison settled on the sofa next to Zoe and Oscar laid his big head in her lap.

Peter handed each of the ladies a bottled water. Viktor knew what he was doing when he grabbed Zoe. She was his weak spot. He would have done anything to save her. Died for her.

Oscar lifted his head and woofed.

"Nate." Madison rose and gave her husband's hand a quick squeeze. "Jeannie." The women shared a hug. Rafe trailed the two detectives.

"How are you feeling, Zoe?" Nate said. "Well enough to tell us what happened?"

Zoe nodded.

Nate and Jeannie settled and prepared to take notes.

"Viktor's men overpowered me while one of them distracted Eric out front."

"What about the clerk?"

"He went out to help Eric." Zoe took a drink of water and screwed the cap back on.

"What did Liska want?"

"To talk to Peter." Her eyes found his. "He said he wanted to get the man who double-crossed him. But I didn't believe him. I thought he meant to kill Peter. I refused to call at first."

"What changed your mind?" Nate said.

"I realized Rafe could trace my phone. I knew they'd rescue me." A grateful smile lifted the corners of her mouth. "And I was right."

"Okay. I'll let you give any details about the men and the van to Detective Jansen." Nate motioned for Rafe and Peter to follow him to the kitchen.

Liska, the professional killer, let her live—like he promised. Maybe what he'd said was true. There was one person Peter needed to talk to—his dispatcher. But how without giving his location away?

Once out of earshot of the women, Nate turned to Peter.

"What did Viktor Liska want to talk about?"

"He claims to have been double-crossed." Peter pulled out a chair at the table. "The itinerary was a plant, and someone arranged for me to pick him up at the airport in order to discredit us both." He rubbed his neck. "His alternate theory is I'm part of the conspiracy against him. In which case, I'm one of his targets."

"Is there any proof to what he claims?"

"Possibly." Peter straightened. "There was a doorman at the hotel where I dropped Liska off who looked a lot like one of the

Homeland Security men who came to your office. I remember his broken nose."

"That would go along with your idea about someone in the government being behind the assassination," Rafe said.

Peter shared a knowing look with Rafe.

"There's something you're not telling me," Nate said.

"It's nothing." Rafe grabbed a soft drink from the fridge. "Mind if I ...?"

Nate waved his okay. "Just remember which of us carries the badge, my friend."

"I do." Rafe took a swig. "We need to do some research first. If anything pops, you'll be the first to know."

<hr>

PETER WATCHED Nate and Jeannie pull away. His thoughts tumbled over one another like pebbles in a fast-moving stream.

"Peter, in here." Rafe called to him from the family room. "War council."

"Not Zoe." Madison placed the back of her hand to her friend's cheek. "She may have a fever."

"No, please." She took Madison's hand in hers. "I promise to rest after we've talked."

"Peter, get her another water before you sit down." Madison tucked a throw around her. "And a couple of Tylenol."

"Let's start with what we know," Rafe said. "Viktor Liska was hired to assassinate Lawrence Merton before he told the world about the fraud going on in Afghanistan. Now it seems like the same men who hired Liska decided to take care of two problems at once by fingering Liska and bringing Peter into the mix. Maybe they think he knows as much as Merton."

"They were the guys who beat up my grandma and tried to kill us on the way back home. Not Liska."

"It looks that way." Rafe paced in front of the couch. "We

need to find who hired Liska. First we talk to your Army buddy, David Underwood, again."

Peter rubbed a hand over his head. "Do we know where he's staying?"

"Not yet, but it's only a matter of time." Rafe sat on a chair by Zoe. "Tomorrow I want you to make a list of what we need from the hardware store."

"I don't need to call," Zoe said. "I'll be fine to go."

Rafe shook his head. "No way. This time we do it my way. Eric and another of my guys will get the stuff. You help install it."

"Do you have any contacts in St. Louis?" Peter said.

"Yeah. Why?"

"Get someone to talk to the dispatcher at the taxi firm where I worked." Peter narrowed his eyes. "He's the one who sent me to the airport to pick up Liska."

"You think he got paid?"

Peter nodded. "And I'd like to know by whom."

A piercing alarm shook the walls.

33

Madison pushed Zoe to the floor, and Peter covered them with his body. Madison maneuvered herself to relieve pressure on her stomach. Rafe yanked his cell phone out of his pocket. He pressed a few buttons, and the screeching stopped.

"Stay low." Peter joined Rafe at the windows.

Madison and Zoe sat.

"Are you okay?" Madison said to her friend.

Zoe nodded. "You?"

"Yes."

They crawled to a window and peeked out. The sun, low in the sky, cast shadows and made it hard to detect a threat.

"Movement at nine o'clock." Rafe drew his gun and spoke into his phone.

Madison tensed. One of Liska's men? Zoe's uncle?

A swarm of men appeared from the shadows converging on the figure of a young man.

Rafe stood. "Bring him in here."

A gust of evening autumnal air wafted in as the heavily armed men in black pulled the boy inside.

"Mrs. Zuberi?"

A young voice made shriller by fear.

"It's me, Tommy Jansen."

Tommy? Madison popped to her feet and rushed into the kitchen. Jeannie would be so excited to see her son. So would Nate.

"Do you know this kid?" Rafe glowered at the frightened teenager.

"Yes." Madison's fingers closed around her silver cross. "May I speak with him alone? He's no threat."

Dirty. Too thin. Clothes torn. She'd expected that. But his missing tooth brought tears to her eyes.

"Would you like something to eat?"

"Got any vanilla ice cream?" he said. "With chocolate syrup?"

"Coming up." Old enough to be considered a legal adult, but still just a boy at heart.

Madison spooned a couple of scoops into a bowl, paused, and put in two more. She set the bowl and the bottle of syrup in front of Tommy and took a seat.

"Where have you been?"

"In the big city. Cincinnati." He shoveled a bite into his mouth.

Madison folded her hands in her lap. "Why'd you leave, Tommy?"

"I—" He stirred his spoon around the bowl. "I messed up. Started hanging out with some guys I thought were cool. When it got bad, I split." He shifted in his chair. "Can I have a drink of water?"

"Sure." Madison handed him a bottle from the frig. "Well, I'm glad you're home."

"Not sure my mom will feel the same." He took a swig.

"She will." Madison sat. "You know her. It's hard for her to show her feelings but trust me, her heart is broken."

He looked up. "I didn't mean to ..."

"It's okay. Hearts mend. Is that why you came here instead of going straight home? Because you weren't sure of how your mom would react?"

"No." He laid his spoon down. "I need to tell you and Captain Zuberi something important."

"Let me get him so he can hear it firsthand." Madison picked up her phone.

"Does Mom have to come with him?" His lower lip quivered, and tears shimmered in his dark eyes.

"Your mom has spent days searching for you. She's sick with worry."

Rafe and his men could easily restrain the boy until Nate and Jeannie got there, but she hoped Tommy would decide to face his mom on his own. *Lord, give me the words to help him make the right decision.*

"Wouldn't you rather see your mom now with the rest of us around for support?"

"I guess so." He pushed his bowl away and slumped in his chair.

Oscar, nails clicking on the wood floor, walked to Tommy and nudged his arm until the young man finally bent to pet him. As always, her sweet dog seemed to sense who needed comforting the most. Soon the boy was on the floor, arms circling Oscar's neck, and his face buried in his fur.

They stayed wrapped together on the floor until a car screeched to a halt in the drive. Tommy sighed and returned to his chair. Oscar remained by his side.

Madison braced for Jeannie's normal blustery entrance. But it never came. Nate entered the room first and kissed Madison on the head. Jeannie hesitated in the doorway.

Tears ran down Madison's cheeks as she watched Jeannie cross the room and pull her son into her arms. They remained locked together for several minutes. Tommy, a couple inches taller than his mother, clung to her like the rock she was and had been throughout his life. Jeannie pushed him to arm's length and took stock of his condition. She ran a hand through his brown hair.

"You need a bath, kiddo." Then she hugged him again.

Finally, apart he grabbed her hand. "Mom, I'm sorry." Tears traced a path through the grime on his face.

"I know." Jeannie scrubbed tears from her cheeks with the palm of her hand. "But—" She pulled him close. "There will be consequences for what you put your dad and me through. You get that, right?"

"Yeah."

"For now, we need you to tell us what you know."

Jeannie pulled a chair close to her son.

"I overheard two men talking about—"

"First of all, where was this?" Nate said.

"In a park in Cincinnati."

"They didn't know you were there?"

Tommy flushed. "I ... was going to ask them for money. I started following them, but when I caught the words Pleasant Valley, I decided to hang back and listen. They sat on a bench, and I got behind them in some trees."

"Quick thinking." Nate smiled at the young man. "Where were you when you first saw them?"

"They were coming out of the Marriott hotel down by the river."

"The AC Hotel?"

"Yeah."

"Can you describe them?"

"The one guy was tall and blond, and he acted like he owned the place." Tommy shrugged. "I thought he might give me a couple dollars. He looked rich."

Madison stiffened. The same description Peter gave her of David Underwood.

"The other guy was just a guy. Average."

"You couldn't see his hair color or whether he had any facial hair?"

"No beard or anything." Tommy shook his head. "He was wearing one of those caps—like dad used to wear when he had his sports car."

"You mean his flat cap? The one where the cap came out over the brim and looked like a triangle on his head?"

"Yeah, that one."

"Okay. We can come back to them later." Nate made some notes. "What did they say?"

"The average guy said to the blond guy 'I think we have a mutual interest in Pleasant Valley' or something like that." Tommy scratched the side of his face. "I decided to find out what they were talking about."

"So, they went to a park bench. Then what?"

"The guy in the cap said he saw the blond guy with Rafe and knew he was looking for a friend of Rafe's. Then the guy in the cap said he was looking for someone connected with Rafe too. He said, 'maybe they could kill two birds with one stone' and he laughed." Tommy shuddered. "It was not a ha-ha laugh if you know what I mean."

"How did the blond man answer?"

"He asked who the guy in the cap was looking for."

"And?"

"The guy in the cap said Zoe Poole."

34

Three pairs of ears listened from the shadows of the family room as Tommy spoke to Nate and Jeannie. Zoe and Peter sat beside each other on the couch with Rafe in the armchair next to them. When Zoe heard her name, she reached for Peter's hand.

"How did the blond man respond?" Nate said.

"The last thing I heard was the blond guy saying, 'I think you have the wrong idea.' Somebody spotted me and I left."

"That's good for now." A chair scooted across the floor. "I'll drive you and your mom back to the station so you can get home. Come in tomorrow morning to give a more detailed statement. Wait here a minute."

Nate entered the family room, his face grim. "I know you all heard what was said. I'm dropping them off at the station, and then I'll be back. I expect you to be here ready to fill me in on the whole story." He nodded and left.

Zoe leaned on Peter's shoulder. He put his arm around her and gathered her to his side.

"It's better this way. Nate's a good guy," Peter said.

"I know. That's not it." Warmth radiated off Peter and her body relaxed. So tired. She stifled a yawn.

Madison rejoined her friends. "Nate should be back in about an hour. Zoe, why don't you lie down? Come on." She helped her to her bedroom.

Zoe curled onto her side. Tears trickled down her face. Uncle Harry would never give up. He wanted her dead. But she was only part of the equation. For him to get the money, her mom had to die too. She bolted out of bed and touched her tattoo. *He promises to protect her mom too.*

She glanced at the clock. Half an hour before she would tell Captain Nate Zuberi her story. Half an hour before she would beg him to help protect her mother.

PETER STOOD when Zoe entered the kitchen. Hair brushed. Face washed and a fresh T-shirt. She'd taken time to prepare herself for what was coming.

"I thought I heard a car in the drive." Zoe retrieved a water from the fridge and sat at the table.

Oscar raised his head and woofed.

"I guess you did." Madison pulled a casserole from the oven.

Nate stopped in the doorway. He wore a don't-mess-with-me frown on his face above a jaw covered with dark bristles, and his shirt was stained with today's on-the-go lunch. Dark hair furrowed from fingers plowed through it too many times.

"I feel like I walked into a movie half-way through," Nate said. "I hate that."

"Sit down, sweetheart." Madison took his arm. "Let me get you some iced tea."

Peter waited while Nate got settled.

"You know most of my story," Peter said. "Except about David Underwood, Senator Carl Underwood's son."

"I'm listening."

"David is an old Army buddy, and the only other man I trust —or did trust."

"What do you mean did?"

"I sent him a copy of the itinerary." Peter collected his thoughts. "David contacted Rafe looking for me. Rafe met with him while I listened in. Even though I said to open the packet on news of my death, he'd opened it anyway."

"You think he may have been the one to leak it to the authorities?"

"I don't know." Peter put his head in his hands. "But the description from Tommy of the blond man fits David."

Nate patted his shirt pockets. "Madison, would you get my phone from my jacket please?" When she nodded, he took her hand. "Let me finish and then we can eat." He glanced at Zoe. "Yours is the story I haven't heard."

"Can I say something?" Rafe raised a hand.

"Go on."

"I'm the one to blame for keeping you in the dark about anything. But before you go off on me, no crime was committed."

"I'll take that into consideration." Nate's face darkened to a glower.

Two determined men. Both on the side of justice in their own way. Rafe was his friend, but his respect for Nate continued to grow daily.

Zoe's voice captured Peter's attention once more.

"The other man Tommy saw was my Uncle Harry. Harry Robinson," Zoe said. "He's after my mom's half of the inheritance from my grandparents."

"The shooting at the impound lot I had you investigate?" Rafe said. "He was shooting at Zoe, not Peter."

"You lied to me," Nate said.

"Not exactly. I just didn't correct you when you assumed it was Peter."

"Same thing, Rafe." Nate tapped the table with a finger. "And you know it."

"Okay." Rafe raised both hands. "You're right."

"What else?"

"We think he was behind my accident. although we can't prove it, and my uncle left a threatening note at my cabin." Zoe took in a deep breath. "He shot my fox with an arrow."

"Pardon me?"

"I have two foxes who live under my porch. I rescued them as cubs." She clasped her hands in front of her. "Peter and I found the female shot in the back with an arrow the same time we found the note."

"Trespassing. Threatening bodily harm. Conspiring to commit bodily harm." Nate noted. "Any evidence?"

"I'll send you the video from Zoe's cameras and give you what we have from the note and the arrow," Rafe said.

Madison chimed in. "I can do a sketch of Zoe's uncle for distribution."

"People, I'm not the only one in danger." Zoe jumped to her feet, knocking her chair over. "My mom is too." She turned to Nate. "I need your help."

"Where is she?"

"She's in a memory care facility in Cincinnati. I'll text you the address." Zoe's hand shook as she took her phone from her pocket.

"I don't have jurisdiction in the city, but I'll arrange for the police to keep an eye on the place." He punched in a number. "You and Madison get me the drawing to give the Cincinnati patrols for an APB. We'll check to see if he has a record or any outstanding warrants."

Peter righted Zoe's chair and scooted it over to her. He hadn't thought about her mom. A man like her Uncle Harry who needed money to satisfy his habits and justified any means to get it wouldn't have the patience to wait for his sister to die a natural death. But ...

"I think you'll still be his main target," Peter said. "Your uncle knows if you die first, he will inherit the money from your mom. But if your mom dies first, he has no idea who inherits from your will. You could leave all of it to the national society to preserve foxes. If there is such a thing."

Relief warmed her eyes and lifted the corners of her mouth. For a moment, everything else blurred around him, and Peter knew the real reason he'd come to Pleasant Valley—Zoe Poole.

"Is there anything else you're forgetting to tell me?" Nate consulted his notes. "If I have this straight, we're looking for Viktor Liska in connection with the shooting of Lawrence Merton and the kidnapping of Zoe. Looking for Harry Robinson for the charges already stated. And for David Underwood as a possible connection to Viktor Liska. Anything more?"

"If David ordered the assassination, he may be after me and have been behind taking my grandmother too." Peter leaned against the kitchen counter.

"But no proof. Nothing from the memory stick?"

Peter forgot about the flash drive. What was it he found before Zoe'd been kidnapped?

"We're working on it." Peter glanced at Rafe.

"Okay." Nate put his phone on the table. "Let's eat and get some sleep. Something tells me tomorrow will be a busy day."

* * *

MADISON STARED at her kitchen table covered with dirty dishes. When had she gone from being an intelligent, thinking woman with a career to chief cook and bottle washer?

She missed teaching chemistry, mostly her students. The look on their faces when it all started to make sense—when they saw the details come together into the larger intricate pattern— the pattern that reflected the hand of the Creator. One advantage to teaching in a Christian school.

Not that she didn't enjoy her present job. She still did chemistry in her lab downstairs, but it was different. Analyzing blood samples and other bodily fluids, lifting fingerprints from varied surfaces, and other forensic procedures.

But sometimes she missed the people interaction—those *aha* moments when a student finally understood a concept, the class jokes that sprung from silly incidents during the year, and the questions that forced her to stretch her own intellect.

To be honest, most of the teenage girls she taught just wanted to get through the class and move on. But every once in a while, there was one ...

Madison placed a stack of dishes in the sink and turned on the faucet. She opened the dishwasher. As she rinsed the plates, fat tears rolled down her face and plopped into the greasy water in the sink.

"Why don't you leave those till tomorrow." Nate opened the refrigerator.

"Who do you think's going to do them tomorrow? Certainly not you. You have a job to do." Madison swiped a wet hand under her running nose. "Besides, we don't have any silverware for breakfast."

She stopped loading the dishwasher and closed her eyes. She was being unfair. "I'm sorry, Nate."

"What's going on?" He turned her to face him.

He'd showered and changed into sweats and a T-shirt. A curl fell over his forehead as his hair dried. She reached for it. He caught her hand.

"Tell me." He pulled her closer. "Is it this case? Rafe? Me?"

"I ... I'm feeling underappreciated I guess." She wrapped her arms around him. "Like all I'm good for is cooking meals and cleaning up."

"Haven't you been doing all the forensics for Rafe?"

"Most of it."

"The job takes skill." Nate captured her eyes with his. "There's more to what's going on."

"I'm signed up for my first graduate chemistry course next semester. How am I going to take a class with a baby?" Where had that come from?

"Ahh. Now I understand." Nate rubbed his thumb across her

cheek. "You're scared about how a baby will change not just your life, but your identity."

He was right. But she wanted this child. She placed a hand on her stomach. "I feel so ashamed." She buried her face against his chest.

"Why?" He stroked her back. "Don't you think I struggle with those thoughts too? Or do you think because I'm the dad and will go off to work each day that having a new baby in my life won't affect me?"

"I won't lie to you. Our baby will change our lives. But I believe for the good. And as far as I'm concerned, you will always be the same beautiful, intelligent, strong woman I married. Who happens to have great cooking and cleaning skills too."

She laughed, pushed away from him, and punched him on the arm. "I need some tissues."

He handed her a box. "Feel better?"

"Yes."

"We'll make this work." Nate grabbed some glasses off the table. "For tonight, I'll help you finish cleaning up this mess so we can go to bed. I'm bushed."

Madison wrapped her fingers around the silver cross at her neck. *Thank You, Father.*

"And text Zoe and the guys. They're on their own tomorrow for breakfast." Nate winked at her.

35

Madison nestled into her favorite rocker on her screened porch. A push with her socked feet set the chair into motion with a slow rhythm. The morning air held promise of a crisp autumn day. If only life could stay just like this.

"You have the best view of the lake from here." Rafe sat on the loveseat, Oscar's head in his lap.

"I know."

"How're you feeling?"

"Fine." She stopped rocking. "Why?"

Rafe kept his eyes straight ahead. "No reason. Just ... you know."

"What I know is you've never asked me how I'm feeling before. What's up?"

He cut his eyes to her. "I don't want to be the cause of any problems between you and Nate."

"You're not." She set the chair in motion again. "Silly."

"After last night, and the text about breakfast ..." Rafe shrugged. "Anyway."

Oscar's head came up.

A man came into sight on the path along the lake. A young brown and white dog ran up Ed and Sarah's yard to the house.

The man whistled. He pressed something in his hand and the dog immediately returned to his side.

An average-looking young man. Wearing black rimmed glasses, a plaid shirt, and a ballcap from MIT. Who was he?

Oscar jumped to the floor and went to the window. A growled sounded low in his throat.

Rafe glanced at his watch. "Right on time."

The dog, nose to the ground, ran up the yard to Madison's house, and the whole whistle thing was repeated.

Oscar woofed, but the dog ignored him.

Madison watched as the same behavior happened again and again at each house they passed.

"Why didn't the alarm go off?" Madison said.

"The guy and his dog walk every morning about this time. I decided to shut it off for an hour rather than deal with it."

"Do you know who he is?"

"New guy. William Smith." Rafe motioned to his right. "Bought the house on the end. Works at the university."

"Do Ed or Sarah know him?"

"No, but they wouldn't. He works for IT. I've had him checked out. He's legit."

"IT would have been my guess. From the look of him." Madison's gaze shifted to Oscar standing at the window. "I know, boy. You miss our walks. So do I."

Later, she'd take her sweet dog out back to play in the lake. She scanned the horizon. The sky was filled with puffy white clouds that belonged in a painting, the beginnings of a beautiful day.

"Aunt Sarah and Uncle Ed are going away for a while," Rafe said.

"Was going into hiding your idea? Or theirs?" Madison shook her head. "Never mind. I'm glad they're going."

"I'd send you and Zoe with them if I thought you'd go."

"Stubborn chauvinist."

"Stubborn feminists."

A smile lifted the corners of her mouth. It was good to have friends who cared.

MADISON TOOK Oscar's face in her hands. "You are not to go out of the yard. Understand?"

He licked her nose.

She was never sure if his doggie kisses meant "Yes" or simply "Love you, Mom." She opened the door, and he bolted through and down the deck. Sigh.

Oscar, nose to the ground, followed the path the brown and white dog had taken into the yard. He huffed and squatted occasionally, marking his territory. Madison followed tossing his favorite tennis ball in her hand.

"Are you about finished, dog?" Madison stepped onto her dock and cast a look over her shoulder in time to see Oscar chewing on something. "Hey, you, spit that out." She rushed to his side.

A five pack of sugar-free gum lay scattered on the grass—two pieces missing. She grabbed Oscar and forced his mouth open, praying he hadn't swallowed them. But no such luck.

"Oh, Oscar, you big lug." She snatched the remaining pieces up, grabbed Oscar's collar and pulled him toward the house.

"What's wrong?" Zoe called to her from the deck.

"I need to get Oscar to the vet right away."

"I'll go along. Meet me in front."

Please, Lord, I can't lose my dog. Madison prayed repeatedly. She knew the toxicity of xylitol in dogs—the main ingredient in sugar-free gum.

And she knew if they ingested too much, there was no effective treatment. Sometimes knowledge made it hard to hang on to hope.

"You drive. You know where we're going." Zoe opened the

hatch and motioned Oscar into the car. "I'll keep an eye on him." She handed Madison her purse.

While Madison backed out, she told Zoe what happened. "Did you let Rafe know where we're going?"

"I'll call him now."

A sound from the back drew their attention.

"Oscar threw up," Zoe said.

"I know." Madison pushed the little silver hybrid faster than she'd ever gone. "Call the vet's office and tell them we're coming."

The staff must have been watching for them. As soon as Madison pulled into a space near the door, two assistants rushed out and carried Oscar into the clinic with Madison on their heels.

"Mrs. Zuberi." A girl at the desk stopped her. "We need you to fill out some paperwork."

"Of course." If she could keep her hand from shaking. *Please, Lord, I can't lose my dog.*

ZOE WATCHED through the glass doors as Oscar and Madison rushed into the office. *Lord, heal Oscar.* No way could she sit in there waiting for news. She'd make herself useful cleaning out the car. A roll of paper towels behind the seat and a water spigot on the side of the building was all she needed. Now for a spritz of her mouth freshener into the air to cover the odor.

"You're a hard woman to find."

The viper—Uncle Harry. She swirled and brought her fists up in front of her face.

"Whoa." He backed up. "No need for violence. Can't we just talk?"

"About what?" Zoe lowered her hands a few inches.

"Can we get out of the parking lot?" He walked closer to the building out of sight of the doors.

What was he up to? If he planned to try anything, he was taking a chance in a public place like this. Could he be that desperate?

"Zoe, I'm sorry," he said. "I let the money go to my head. Please."

She dropped her hands and moved closer. "You tried to kill me."

"I—" A tear slid down his cheek. "I don't expect you to forgive me. But I'm glad for the chance to tell you I'm sorry. You won't ever see me again."

"What made you change so fast?" Part of her wanted to believe him. He was her only living relative besides her mother.

"I haven't." He pulled a gun. "I'm just sorry it has to be this way. I did try to talk with you first if you remember." He motioned with the barrel the direction he wanted her to go.

The door to the vet's office opened.

"The vet thinks Oscar has a chance. It's slim, but he—"

Zoe lunged for her uncle. Too late. He swung his gun around. The bullet caught Madison in the chest. Zoe stared in disbelief as her friend flew backward and landed against the wall.

36

Zoe pushed her uncle aside and sprinted to Madison. The girl from the vet's office shoved open the door.

"Call 911." Zoe kneeled next to her friend.

She undid Madison's jacket to expose a bulletproof vest. *Thank You, Jesus.*

Madison groaned. Her eyes fluttered open.

"Don't move." Zoe put a hand on her shoulder. "The ambulance is on its way."

"I feel like I fell off a cliff."

Zoe cocked an eyebrow. "You know what that's like, do you?"

"I bet it feels a lot like this." Madison gave her a weak smile.

"You scared ten years out of me. I thought you were—" Zoe swallowed. "Where did you get the vest?"

"Nate. He insists I wear it whenever I leave the house. Even in the backyard."

"God bless Nate," Zoe said. "And God bless you for doing what he asks."

Madison took a deep breath and grimaced. "Who shot me with the canon anyway?"

Zoe's head snapped up. Uncle Harry. But he'd disappeared from sight.

"Uncle Harry. I was about to be taken to some dark place and killed." Zoe sat on the sidewalk next to Madison. "I owe you. You took a bullet for me, my friend."

Madison closed her eyes. "You'd do the same thing for me."

A siren screamed into the parking lot. A man and a woman quick stepped over to where Madison lay with Zoe by her side.

"We've got it. Thanks."

Efficient. Pleasant, but firm. Get out of their way and let them work. Zoe snagged Madison's purse and moved away. Another siren captured her attention. Nate. She plotted a course to intercept him.

"Where is she?" Nate plowed a path toward the clump of uniforms on the walk.

Zoe put a hand on his arm. "She's fine. The vest saved her."

"She had it on?" He rubbed a finger under his eye.

"Of course, she did. You asked her to."

He closed his eyes and pinched the bridge of his nose. "Good."

The EMTs wheeled Madison toward the ambulance.

"I need to see her." Nate took a step. "Don't go anywhere. We need to talk."

Not a conversation she looked forward to.

———

MADISON LIFTED the oxygen mask away from her face and gave him a weak smile. "I'm fine, Nate. A little sore, but that's all."

"You know she's having a baby?" Nate growled at the attendant. "Our baby."

"Yes, sir." The young man didn't flinch. "She doesn't appear to be hurt other than some bruising on her chest, but we're taking her back to the hospital to have her examined as a precaution."

"See? I'll be fine." Madison touched Nate's hand.

"Give us a minute," Nate said.

The EMT stepped down from the ambulance.

"When I heard you'd been shot—" Nate ran a hand through his hair. "I'm not sure I can live with—"

"Not another word." Madison pinned him with her eyes. "Every day you leave the house, and I don't know if I'll see you again. But I've learned to live with it because you're doing a job you love and it's important.

"The same is true of me. These are the paths we're meant to walk, and we were put together in order to encourage and help each other along the way." She replaced her mask and took a deep breath of oxygen.

He took her hand in his. "I love you, Madison Zuberi."

"I love you too. Now answer your phone, Captain Zuberi."

"It'll wait." He nodded to the EMT.

She tugged on his hand. "Answer it. Somebody needs you."

"You need me."

She shook her head. What she needed was two aspirin and a nap.

"Go."

"Sir, we need to leave."

Nate motioned to an officer nearby. "Go with my wife to the hospital. Guard her like your badge depends on it—because it does."

Madison closed her eyes. *My husband. So protective.* But then, if he wasn't, she wouldn't have been wearing the vest. Her fingers touched the cross at her neck.

ZOE PULLED her hair into a ponytail. She leaned against Nate's car and stared at the asphalt. Every time she tried to organize her thoughts, they lined up nice and neat—until she got to where Madison stepped through the door. Then, like birds on a power line when a hawk flies over, they took off in all directions.

One fact stuck with her like the note arrowed onto her porch. *Madison is pregnant.*

"Stall them as long as you can." Nate stopped in front of her, his phone to his ear. "And check with Homeland Security to see if they really work there." He ended his call.

"The two guys purporting to be from Homeland Security showed up at the precinct with a warrant. They'll try for my house next." Nate massaged his forehead. "We'll have to table our talk for now. I want you to get Peter out of there. Take Madison's car."

"How is she?" Zoe couldn't leave without knowing.

"Bruised, but okay. I'm going to the hospital to get her."

Zoe's knees gave for a split second. *Thank You, Jesus.*

"Did you put out an APB on Uncle Harry? He's probably driving a silver sportscar."

"Done."

Zoe grabbed Madison's purse and jogged to her car.

"Text Rafe where you'll be," Nate called after her.

She already knew where she'd take Peter. Her sanctuary in the woods.

37

"Grab a few things and meet me in the drive. We need to hide. We're going to my place." Zoe tossed her phone on the console between the seats.

She bit her lip. Taking Peter to her cabin seemed like the perfect idea at the time, but now she wasn't so sure. Only a living room, kitchen, bath, and two bedrooms. Was she ready to share her small sanctuary with someone else? Would he get the wrong idea?

Maybe a hotel with separate rooms would be better. But the security at her cabin ...

She pulled into the driveway of the rental. Peter flung two duffle bags in the back and climbed in.

"I brought my sleeping bag so I could encamp in the barn and leave the house for you." He fastened his seatbelt. "I assume we'll eat together, but I don't feel right staying in the house just the two of us. Besides, I know how special your cabin is to you."

It took every ounce of willpower not to kiss him. But she needed to stay on task.

"Thanks." She backed out of the driveway and sped up the street. "Lay the seat back as far as it will go and put this ballcap

183

over your face. We may pass the Homeland Security guys headed this way."

"Maybe I'll take a little nap."

"Yeah. Good idea."

Zoe directed a quick look at the man beside her. Despite her best efforts, Peter had taken up permanent residence in her heart, and it frightened her more than anything Uncle Harry or Viktor Liska said or did to her. Her body would heal, but she wasn't so sure about the damage Peter could inflict to her heart.

As THE CAR SLOWED, Peter took a deep breath and opened his eyes.

"We're here," Zoe said.

He emerged from the car and stretched. The sight of the cabin and Zoe petting her foxes brought peace to his soul. "I'll put my stuff in the barn and join you on the porch." He hated to draw her away from her friends.

"I'll come with you." She rose and swept her eyes over the landscape.

"The door's ajar." Peter dropped his bags and reached for his gun.

"That happens sometimes. I must not have closed it all the way."

"Better safe than sorry." He put out an arm to stop her. "Let me go in first."

He stepped across the threshold. A shadow to his left and a change in air pressure. He twisted in time to miss being hit on the head, but the black baton slammed his wrists, and his gun went flying. Peter whirled to face his opponent. He ducked as the baton barely missed his head.

"Stop, Uncle Harry, or I'll shoot."

Zoe. Peter's heart lurched in his chest.

A shot echoed off the concrete floor and metal sides. It coincided with a thwack of solid on flesh and a scream from Zoe.

Blood pounded in Peter's ears. He sighted in on the man's back, his arm raised to deliver another blow. Peter lowered his head and ran at him. Harry turned at the last second. The solid wood baton came down on Peter's back. Pain shot through his spine and down his legs. But he drove the man through the door and onto the ground outside.

The air left Harry's lungs in a rush, and the nightstick fell from his hand as Peter's weight pinned him to the earth. Peter pushed to his knees, gathered Harry's shirt in his left hand, and cocked his right arm to deliver the first blow.

"No." Zoe grabbed Peter's right bicep. "We've got him." She handed him a pair of handcuffs.

"You are one lucky guy." Peter lifted the cuffed man to his feet. "I guess we better call Nate."

Zoe shook her head. "Nate's busy with other business. I suggest we call Rafe and let him take my uncle into the police station. We can take pictures to send with him and record our statements." A crease formed between her eyes. "But now the barn is a crime scene. Where will you sleep?"

PETER FLEXED his foot to set the rocker in motion. A full belly, a cool breeze, and the constant gurgling of the nearby stream conspired to put him to sleep. His head fell to his chest, and he startled. "Must have dozed off. Sorry."

"Not a problem. It's been a long day." Zoe yawned. "Are you sure you'll be okay in my tent?"

He barked a laugh. "It's a palace compared to some places I've slept."

"I guess it is, isn't it?" Zoe turned toward him. "So, you're okay with me bringing you here instead of getting a couple of rooms at a motel?"

"I'd much rather be here." What's bothering her?

"I thought it would be easier to defend," Zoe said. "Although I'll have to figure out how Uncle Harry got in. There's obviously a gap in my security somewhere."

"We'll find it." He smiled at her. "This is a great place. You're lucky to have it."

"Viktor Liska told me you carry around a picture of a cabin in your pocket," Zoe said. "What's the story there?"

He laid his head back and sighed. "Let's wait until I'm not so tired."

"You know, you're running up quite a tab." She threw him a grin. "There's the one about your scar and now the cabin story. Not to mention the talk we need to have when this is all over."

Peter shook his head. "You don't forget a thing, do you?"

But she was right. It was time he told her how he felt. Why was it easier for him to walk into enemy fire than to deal with the important women in his life? He stood and walked to the porch railing. A blanket of stars drew his gaze. Where should he begin?

"I had been driving cab for about a year when one night, I saw a young man stumbling along the sidewalk. I stopped to help. Offered him a ride. He got in the back, slumped over, and told me an address."

Peter turned to face Zoe. "When I got there, I reached in to help him out, and he pulled a knife. Sliced my face then held it to my throat and robbed me." Peter put a finger to his cheek. "Blood ran down my face, my arm, drenched my shirt. I was a real mess. I guess I was in shock because I didn't even fight back. Just got in my cab and drove to the nearest hospital."

She moved close to him and ran her soft fingers down his scar. "Thank you for telling me." Her magnificent violet eyes caressed his face as if she could see his whole life written in every shadow, wrinkle, and crag. Maybe she could. Maybe that's what love does to people. Like a secret code only they can read.

He pulled her close and placed his mouth to her ear. "When

I saw your uncle standing over you ... I could have killed him with my bare hands." His lips found hers while his fingers wove a path deep into her mane of hair at the back of her neck. Their kiss deepened as she pressed against him. Fire shot through his body. He needed to pull away before their passion took over. *I need Your strength, Lord.* With a thudding heart, he released her and took a step back.

"It's late. We really should get some rest." Peter touched her cheek.

She smoothed a hand over his T-shirt. "You still owe me the story about the cabin."

"Tomorrow." He took her shoulders and turned her toward the door. "Inside. Lock the doors and windows."

"Why? I never lock—"

"Just do it." Peter gave her a gentle push. "Please."

Peter waited on the porch until he heard the locks click into place on the door. He walked around the cabin following Zoe's silhouette in the windows as she did as he had asked. When he was satisfied she was secure, he returned to the porch and folded his north-of-six-foot frame into the rocker as best he could. It was going to be a long night.

38

Madison grimaced for what must have been the hundredth time that morning. Thankfully, the bullet hadn't broken any ribs. The bruising was painful enough. She eased into a chair at the table and stirred a sugar substitute into her tea.

The doorbell chimed. She glanced at her phone. Probably the young man who cuts their grass wanting to be paid. She rose with a groan, walked into the living room, and opened the door.

"Who are you?" Madison appraised the two men on her porch. "And what do you want?" Dark blue suits like government officials perhaps, but their shoes—scuffed and worn.

"We're from Homeland Security." The taller man flipped an identification wallet at Madison.

These were the two she'd heard about. The tall one and the one with the broken nose. Strange. Just the two. No backup. She examined them more closely. Thin brown hair with a receding hairline showed above sunglasses perched on the broken nose. The other man, the taller one, kept his hat on. Probably bald. He smiled at her. Brown teeth. A smoker or too much coffee?

"We have a warrant to search your premises."

The sound of a car drew Madison's attention. Nate, thank God.

"My husband, Captain Nate Zuberi is home. You can deal with him."

"Don't let them in, Madison." Nate strode across the lawn.

"I didn't intend to."

"I did some checking on you two," Nate said. "Homeland Security has no record of either of you."

"Your village police department doesn't know how to spell Homeland Security."

"But my FBI friend does." Nate pointed a finger at them. "You're bogus and so is your warrant."

Madison gritted her teeth. Why did so many people think small towns were backward?

"You're making a big mistake." The men backed away. "We will find Peter Grace. With or without your help."

"Not here you won't," Nate said. "Get off my property before I throw you in jail for trespassing."

The two men tromped across the yard to their car. Tall man wedged himself behind the steering wheel and they took off up the street.

Madison glowered as she watched their car drive off. "I wish Oscar had been here. He would have bitten them."

Nate shook his head. "Then we would have had a lawsuit on our hands."

She turned into his arms. "I'm so glad you showed up when you did."

Clouds covered the sun and fat raindrops spattered the sidewalk and left dark spots on Nate's jacket. A light wind blew by, and she shivered.

"I'd hoped to get here ahead of them." Nate put an arm around her waist and led her inside. "I don't think we've seen the last of them, but hopefully it'll be a while before they show up again. Where's Eric?"

"He's running an errand for Rafe." Madison rubbed her arms. "Do you think it's okay for Peter and Zoe to come back?"

"Let's give it a day," Nate said. "I want to find out more about those two guys." He kissed her on the cheek. "I need to get back. Will you be okay here?"

"Yes. Eric should be back soon."

"I'll call later." He headed out the door.

"Their shoes were wrong, Nate."

"What?"

"They had on scuffed black lace-up chukka boots. Not the kind of shoes you wear with a suit."

"Good catch, sweetheart." He smiled at her and climbed into his car.

She managed a smile and fought back the wave of sadness threatening to pull her under. The clouds outside couldn't compare to the clouds inside her heart right now. Down in the dumps is what her mom called it. Sarah left with Ed for a week. Zoe and Peter were hiding out. Rafe was buried in computer work. Oscar was sick.

Nate asked her to stop going to Bible study and out to lunch for a while until they caught Viktor Liska and the man who hired him. Her bruised chest hurt, and she missed her friends and her dog.

She headed for her screened porch and the solace of her rocker and Bible. But as she entered, she spied the new guy, William Smith, and his brown and white dog coming her way along the path. If he hadn't been so careless, Oscar wouldn't be so sick. She blinked away tears of anger and pushed through the screened door.

Madison planted herself on the path, arms crossed in front of her, and waited for him to approach. He stopped about ten feet away.

"Is there a problem?" He grabbed the collar of his dog. "My understanding was that the path was open for common use."

"It is." Madison put as much ice in her voice as she could. "But I have a big problem when your carelessness puts my dog in the hospital fighting for his life."

"Excuse me?"

"The sugar-free gum you dropped."

"Miss, I do not chew gum." The chill in his voice matched her own. "And if I did, I would be especially careful with it since I am a dog owner as well."

She was so sure Smith had been the culprit. Would he have done it on purpose to harm Oscar? If so, he took a chance. His own dog could be the one on death's door.

"I'm sorry." Madison let her hands drop to her side. "I'm just worried about my dog."

His brown and white dog broke away from him and ran toward Madison. She bent to pet him, but Smith blew his whistle and called him back.

"Please don't pet him. He's in training."

She straightened. "Training for what?"

"To be a sniffer dog."

"For drugs?"

Smith looked at his watch. "I need to go. Work." He snapped a leash on his dog and gave her a cold stare. "I'm sorry about your dog."

She rubbed her arm as a breeze with the hint of winter touched her skin. His eyes were like black holes in a face with neither frown lines nor laugh lines to show his character. A man without feelings. He wasn't sorry for Oscar.

A man who needed prayer. Madison returned to her screened porch and her rocker and Bible.

PEACE RESTORED TO HER SOUL, Madison turned her thoughts to food. What to fix for dinner? Chicken or hamburgers? Or she could use the hamburger to make meatballs for spaghetti? That—

She cocked her head. Did she hear the front door? She thought she locked it. Maybe Eric had arrived. But wouldn't he call out to her like he usually did? She slid out of the rocker and crawled from the screened porch into the kitchen. If it was Eric, he'd have a good laugh and she'd have to take some pain meds, but if not …

A floorboard squeaked in the living room. Whispered conversation set every nerve in her body on edge. She'd placed her gun in a drawer in the blue cupboard in the kitchen. She tiptoed along the floor careful not to bump into any furniture. At the cupboard, she eased the drawer open. Despite her best efforts, the antique wood protested with a small screech.

Madison yanked on the drawer and withdrew her gun as the two supposed Homeland Security men appeared in the doorway from the living room. She crouched and aimed.

"Stop or I'll shoot."

The man with the broken nose reached for his firearm.

"Don't, you idiot," his partner said.

Madison pulled the trigger. Eyes wide with surprise, the man fell to the floor. His partner, the tall man, turned and ran.

Madison pushed a kitchen chair out of the way and walked to the fallen man.

"Don't move." She kicked his gun away and fought to keep her aim steady, but her hands seemed to have a will of their own.

"Madison, give me the gun." Rafe came up behind her and slid his hands over hers. "I'll take it from here."

She released her grip and collapsed into a nearby kitchen chair, clutching her hands in her lap to keep them from shaking. "Is he dead?"

"No. He'll live." Rafe felt through the man's pockets. He laid the man's cell phone on the table. "See if you can find anything on his phone. Use gloves."

Good. A task to focus on. "It's password protected, but I can pull up the number." Familiar somehow. But how? She made note of it.

"We'll put it back for now. Let the police do their thing." He replaced the phone in the man's pocket. "I have photos of his ID and other items in his wallet. Time to call Nate."

"What about the other guy?"

"He's outside. Resting."

Madison would need another session with her rocker after this. She grabbed a soft drink from the refrigerator. The cold can felt good against her brow. She closed her eyes for a moment then stared at the phone number again. Why was it so familiar?

"Does this mean anything to you?" She held the paper out for Rafe to read.

"No." He studied it for a moment. "It's a D.C. number."

Of course. Madison rushed to her lab. She returned with the itinerary from Peter. "It's one digit away from the number off the itinerary."

Their gaze was drawn to the man lying on her kitchen floor.

"Who is this guy?" she said.

"Good question," Rafe said. "Maybe we should wake him up."

Rafe kneeled beside the stricken man. He shifted the man's head. A groan escaped his lips.

"Wake up. We need to talk."

The blare of sirens grew closer.

Rafe slapped the man's cheek. "Who do you work for?"

The man's mouth gaped open. Bloody drool dripped onto Rafe's hand.

Madison touched Rafe's shoulder. "Enough. The police are here. Leave him alone." The man was in pain. He wouldn't have hesitated to hurt her, but it made no difference.

Rafe washed his hands at the sink while Madison met the EMTs at the door. The tall man sat in handcuffs on the porch step, and other emergency techs checked him over. Police swarmed over the lawn and into the house bringing back bad memories from two years ago.

"There you are." Nate enfolded her in his arms.

She breathed out her anxiety and inhaled the smell of his aftershave mixed with wool from his jacket. *Thank You, Jesus, for this man.*

"I'm so sorry, sweetheart." He stroked her hair.

"You had no way of knowing they'd be back so soon."

Nate studied her face. "How are you?"

"If I'd killed him ..." She shrugged. "But since he'll make it, I'm okay."

"You'll still need to see a counselor for a few sessions. Shooting a person is very traumatic. We'll set you up with one."

"At least now you can hold them for breaking and entering." She cocked her head. "I was sure I locked the front door. How did they get in?"

"Picked the locks. And I've got them for a lot more than B and E. They knew you were home." Nate's face hardened. "Maybe now we'll find out who they're working for."

"The one—" Oops.

"What?"

She played with his lapel. "Promise you won't get mad."

"Madison, what have you done now?"

"Rafe and I tried to open the cell phone of the guy I shot." She raised pleading eyes to his. "We couldn't get inside, but we got the number. And we realized something important."

Nate closed his eyes, his lips silently moving. She wasn't sure if he was praying or counting to ten.

"What did you find?"

"The number on his phone is only one digit away from the one on the itinerary Peter brought with him."

"A possible connection between these two and the assassination." Nate nodded. "That *is* important."

He smoothed some hair off her cheek. "You look tired."

"I am." She yawned.

"By the way, Harry Robinson is in custody. He made another

attempt on Zoe's life at her cabin, and she and Peter caught him."

Some of the clouds in her heart parted and let hope shine through. Maybe life would soon be back to normal, and she could bury the past once again.

39

Peter slouched in the rocker, eyes closed. He sensed someone staring at him. Without moving a muscle, he mentally prepared himself to attack. Slitting his right eye to sight in on his enemy, he experienced a moment of confusion. No one in sight.

He lowered his view. Zoe's two foxes sat in front of him, heads cocked in a questioning way as if to say, "Don't you belong inside?"

Peter pushed himself up in the chair. The animals shot down the steps and under the porch. "I'm harmless. Promise." He stretched.

"I'm not too sure about that." Zoe stepped outside.

"At least to foxes." He grinned.

She handed him a steaming mug. "Did you sleep here all night?"

"Guilty." Peter took a sip. Hot coffee slid down his throat and pressed the starter button to his brain.

"Why? Uncle Harry's in jail."

"But he could have an accomplice. And there's still Liska and his boss to think about." He stood, tossed his blanket on the rocker, and set his cup down. "I don't take chances."

"How about showers? Do you take those? Would you like to take one while I make breakfast?"

"Funny." He grabbed her and planted a kiss on her lips. One kiss turned into a few kisses before he disengaged from her.

Zoe didn't move, lips parted and a soft look in her eyes.

"I'm going to take my shower now. I'll use the outside one I saw by the barn."

Halfway to the barn, a vibration in his jeans pocket got his attention. Unknown caller.

"Grace."

"Peter. My friend."

"I told you before, Liska, you're not my friend." Peter tightened his grip on the phone. "What do you want?"

"Same as before. To talk. I have questions and answers, my —Peter."

"I haven't had breakfast yet. Give me an hour." Peter peered at his phone. "You'll have to call me back since I don't know your number."

"Yes. But do not bother with a trace. I am careful."

PETER WIPED his hands on his pants. Somehow the call from Liska didn't make him as nervous as his first time entering Zoe's home. What's with that? He knocked on the frame of the screen door.

"Come on in."

The minute he stepped inside, his jitters disappeared. He felt at home surrounded by the soft gleam of wood. The stone fireplace and the comfortable couch and chairs beckoned him to sit with one of the many books tucked on shelves covering the walls. But smells from the kitchen beyond drew him on.

Zoe placed a bowl of scrambled eggs and a platter of bacon on the scarred oak table.

"Here you go." She held up the coffeepot. "More?"

"Sure." He let his eyes rove over the open shelves in the kitchen with mismatched crockery that somehow fit together and glasses of all colors and sizes. "It fits you."

"What does?"

"Your house." He swept his arm in an arc.

"Thanks." She grinned. "I love it here."

Peter pushed some egg around on his plate. "I got a call from Viktor Liska. He wants to talk." He looked across the table at her. "I told him to call back in an hour, and I asked Rafe to be here when he does."

She laid her fork down. "How much time to we have?"

"Maybe fifteen minutes."

She sighed. "I guess we'd better eat fast."

Another knock on the door.

"I'll get it." Peter pushed away from the table. Rafe stood outside the screen door. "Thanks for coming. I don't hold out much hope for tracing his call but thought we might as well try."

"Where should I set up?"

"In here." Zoe motioned them into the kitchen.

She'd cleared the table and poured two cups of coffee.

"Plug your phone in here." Rafe keyed in a few numbers. "When he calls, keep him on as long as you can."

Peter nodded.

Rafe's phone rang. He looked at the screen and then at Peter and Zoe, bringing a finger to his lips, he pushed speaker.

"Rafe? Are you there?"

"David. You disappeared without telling me how to get in touch with you."

"I know. I realized that later. Have you heard anything?"

Rafe stared at Peter. "Yes. But I don't trust the phones. We need to meet."

"Same place?"

"No. Where are you?"

Hesitation. "In Cincinnati. Pleasant Valley's too small for me."

"Where are you staying?" Rafe motioned to Peter to make a note.

"The AC Marriott down by the water. But I don't want to meet here. It's too crowded."

Rafe's lips pressed together for a moment. "Let me get back to you about a meeting place. Where can I reach you?"

"I'll text you the number."

Rafe pushed the end call button.

"Would David give you his number if he's involved with this mess?" Nervous energy demanded release. Peter needed to move. He took his cup to the kitchen sink.

"He could afford to if he switched phones right after," Zoe said.

"True."

Rafe's phone buzzed with a text. He stared at it. "What if I set the meeting for the rental?"

"The rental?" Zoe jumped to her feet. "Isn't that dangerous?"

"Where would you suggest? Here?"

She touched the cabin wall next to her. "No."

"What do you think?" Rafe glanced at Peter.

"Should we alert Nate?" And what about Madison? He didn't want anyone else hurt because of him.

"Good question."

An alarm sounded on Zoe's phone. "The police forensics people are here. I'll let them in." She left the house.

"Let's do it. I want this to be over with." Peter touched his shirt over his tattoo. He would lean on His promises of protection and strength for all of them.

Rafe nodded.

Peter's phone rang. Unknown caller. "It's Liska."

"I have been trying to get through."

"You've got me now. What do you want?"

The screen door opened with a screech. Zoe stepped inside. "They—"

Rafe ran a hand across his neck and pointed to Peter.

"Who am I hearing in the room with you?" Liska said.

"Zoe. I'll tell her to leave."

"No, no. How is the lovely Zoe doing? Please tell her I am so sorry for treating her so poorly."

"Get to the point, Liska."

"I need to know how close you are to your friend from Washington, and please do not say his name over the phone."

"Why?"

"Answer the question please."

"We served in the Army together. We became friends. But I haven't seen him for four or five years."

"I know he is in town looking for you." Liska said. "And he had lunch with your friend Rafe the other day."

"You were there too."

"I think you do not trust your old friend, and you are right to feel this way."

"Why?" Peter drew a shallow breath, ears tuned to what Liska would say next.

"Because—"

Zoe's alarm sounded again. She checked her monitors. "We've got company. And they're not here to visit." She raced to her bedroom and returned with a revolver and a rifle.

"How many do you see?" Peter hung up his phone and grabbed his gun. How had they found them?

"Six." Rafe switched views from camera to camera. He uttered a mild oath. "Jeannie and Madison are at the barn doing forensics. We need to get them to safety."

Peter's pulse ramped up. "I'll go."

"No. You're the main target. They'll follow you." Rafe shifted to face Zoe. "You know the terrain best."

She pushed her revolver into her waistband and rechecked her rifle.

Peter and Zoe locked eyes for a moment. He watched as his heart walked out the back door with the woman in forest green camo. *Dear God keep her safe.*

40

Zoe slipped through the back door and crouched next to a pine tree. No sign of the intruders. Yet. Any moment, Jeannie or Madison could come through the barn door without knowing the threat that awaited them. Zoe moved from tree to tree until she was within six feet of the barn.

There they were. Men in jeans and ballcaps with automatic rifles advancing on the house, as if they knew Peter was inside. But how? When their attention was on the porch, she crossed the distance to the barn door and slid inside shutting the door behind her.

"Hey." Jeannie swung her flashlight beam on Zoe. "You can't be in here."

"Shh." Zoe placed a finger over her lips. "Get your light out of my eyes. Men are outside after Peter. We need to get you out of here."

"Not me." Jeannie pulled her gun from its holster. "But Madison, yes."

"No. I'll hide, but I'm not leaving." Madison scanned the barn. "Maybe in the hayloft?"

"Not a bad idea. Call Nate and keep out of sight." Jeannie

gave her a gentle push in the direction of the ladder leading to the loft.

"PETER?" Viktor Liska listened to the voices and sounds in the background. Was that an alarm? Company? How many? Peter and Zoe were under attack.

He hung up and dialed a new number. "Why are you not reporting to me what is going on?"

"What are you talking about?" the man said. "Nothing's happening."

"Can you see the lake? No boats?"

"Yes, and no boats."

So where are they? "When did you last see Peter or Zoe?"

"Yesterday Ms. Poole left with Mr. Grace. Let me check the log to see when they returned." The man hummed a tuneless melody. "There's no record of them returning."

"What have you seen today?"

"Mr. O'Connell left this morning, and Mrs. Zuberi left early afternoon. Neither has returned."

They were at the cabin. Zoe's defense systems alarmed when the men approached.

"Gather the others and go directly to the address I text you now. Peter and Zoe are under attack. I will meet you there."

Peter and Zoe would need their help.

If Viktor and his men were not too late.

ZOE SLID the barn door open wide enough to survey the scene outside. A man in a plaid shirt stood several feet away. She held her breath. Had he heard the slight squeak of the door? He turned and for a split second their eyes met. Surprise slowed his reaction enough to give her time to pull the door closed.

He called to the man farther down the yard. Zoe grabbed Jeannie. They raced to the other end of the building and hid behind an old tractor. Bullets tore through the metal siding cutting a murderous line through the cavernous space. Zoe and Jeannie flattened themselves to the floor.

The barn door creaked. A shadow stretched across the concrete floor.

PETER PEEKED out the window in Zoe's bedroom. "What do you see on the monitors?"

"Two bogeys going to our left. Two to our right. Two coming straight in," Rafe said.

"I see the two splitting to the left. Probably going around back." Peter let the curtain fall. "Any suggestions on how we do this?"

"Hang on." Rafe's tone grew urgent. "The two on our right are headed for the barn."

Peter moved quickly to the monitors in time to see the men strafe the side of the barn with gunfire. A growl of rage formed in his throat. He turned, but Rafe caught his arm.

"No. Zoe, Jeannie, and Madison are seasoned and trained. They can handle those two." Rafe tapped some buttons. "But they did give us more of an advantage. Let's get the two coming in the back. Then come around and catch the two in the front from behind."

Peter wrenched his eyes from the window facing the barn and nodded. He checked his gun and ammo. "Let's do this."

Peter crouched at the back door, pushed it open, and peered out. A man in a green shirt and ballcap rounded the corner of the house from his right. Peter sprang through the door and down the steps. Three shots sounded. He landed in a crouch facing his enemy, but the man in the ballcap lay dead. Rafe stood on the porch, gun smoking.

Peter moved close to the house and peeked around the corner. Another man in a gray shirt, back to the wall of the house about six feet away. The man fired, but the shot went high. Rafe moved behind Peter and touched his shoulder.

Peter dove for the ground and fired. The man in the gray shirt fell as Peter's bullets found their mark. Rafe bent to pull Peter to his feet and staggered.

"You okay?" Peter grabbed his friend around the shoulders. His hand felt something sticky. Blood. "You've been shot."

Rafe shrugged. "No big deal."

Peter led him into the shadow of the house. "Let me look at it."

"No." Rafe pushed him away. "We still got four guys out there."

"You said the women could handle two of them."

"Yeah. Well."

Peter sighed. "You are one stubborn soldier."

"Hooah."

Peter glanced at the window above them, and into the face of a man with a beard.

41

"I'll draw their fire." Zoe whispered.

"I should—" Jeannie said.

"Don't argue. You're a better shot."

Zoe spied a gear from the tractor laying on the floor. "I have another plan." She threw the piece of metal as hard as she could across the barn. It hit the side with a clang and drew an automatic reaction from both the men who unloaded their second clips into the corner.

While the men focused in the direction of the sound, Zoe and Jeannie circled behind them. The two men caught the movement at their backs at the last moment and turned. Zoe squared off with the man in the plaid shirt. The other man ran, and Jeannie chased after him.

"Put the gun down or I'll shoot." Zoe pointed her revolver at the man's chest.

He lowered his rifle to the floor and stared at Zoe. He was trying to read her. Would she pull the trigger or not? She wasn't sure herself. She prayed she wouldn't have to find out.

"Turn around and put your hands behind your back." She drew a zip tie from her pocket and stepped closer. She realized her mistake as soon as she was within striking distance. How could she put the tie on him from behind and still hold her gun?

He spun, a chop to her wrist sending her revolver scooting across the floor. Pain. She blocked a blow with her forearm, pivoted, and caught him in the stomach with a kick. He went down with a grunt but bounced to his feet. They moved in a circle facing each other. What was his weakness? Shorter than her but more muscle. Body armor made him less flexible but able to withstand kicks to the torso.

Light from one of the myriad bullet holes arrowed into his eyes and he blinked. Her chance. She swept her leg around knocking him off balance. Her fist punched through the air aimed at his face. But instead of the impact of bone on flesh, her balled hand moved through empty air. His hand grabbed her wrist flipping her over onto her back with a loud whoosh of expelled air. A bolt of pain flashed up her spine as her back landed on the concrete floor.

He landed on top of her, hands at her throat before she could catch her breath. She clawed at his face. If she could reach his eyes. Any tender spot where she could ... Her arms fell to her sides. Strength fading.

A voice in the distance.

"Stop or I'll use this."

A laugh. "You'll kill her too."

"Not if I use it like this." Whack.

Through the slits of her eyes, Zoe saw the butt of the rifle connect with the man's head.

His grip loosened on her neck, but a heavy weight pressed on her chest.

Weight gone. Shuddering breath. Air. Beautiful air.

"Zoe open your eyes."

Madison.

"Good. I need you to help me tie this guy up."

Zoe pushed to her elbows. Plaid shirt guy lay out cold on the concrete with Zoe's rifle several feet away. "Did you?"

"Yes. But hurry. I don't know how long he'll be out."

Zoe pulled zip ties from her back pocket and bound his hands and feet. When she finished, she joined Madison behind the tractor.

"I thought I was dead." Zoe gave her a quick hug. "Thank you, friend."

"It's not over yet." Madison stared across the expanse. "We'll celebrate when we both get through this alive."

"Have you seen Jeannie and the other guy?"

Madison shook her head. "But I heard gunshots." She glanced at Zoe. "I'm praying she's not hurt."

"I'll check." Zoe picked up her rifle and headed for the barn door. Before she made it halfway, the door opened a foot and Jeannie slipped in.

"Thank God, you're okay." Madison rushed to the women.

Jeannie ushered them further into the barn. "There's at least two more out there. Probably more. I don't know where Peter and Rafe are." She looked at Madison. "Did you get through to Nate?"

"I can't get a signal in here."

Zoe and Jeannie pulled out their phones and shook their heads.

"Must be the building." Jeannie tucked her phone back in her pocket.

"What happened to the guy you chased out of here?"

"He got away." Jeannie's mouth set in a grim line. "Listen. This is my job, but Madison, you and Zoe need to stay safe. Stay in here with the prisoner while I try to help the guys."

Zoe shook her head. "If you're going out there, then so am I."

Madison put a hand on her stomach. "Give me a gun and I'll stay here."

Zoe and Jeannie slid the barn door open. The setting sun painted a mosaic of shadows over the ground.

Zoe tapped Jeannie on the shoulder and pointed. One of the

intruders moved cautiously next to the house toward the back. Intent on his destination, he hadn't noticed them.

"Pleasant Valley Police. Stop or I'll shoot." Jeannie strode out of the barn toward the man.

"A cop, huh?" He took cover behind Zoe's stack of firewood and fired at Jeannie. "Here's what I think about cops."

She stepped behind a tree. "Somehow I knew he'd say that."

"What now?" Zoe pressed her back against a slim pine.

"I'm thinking."

A bullet screamed past Zoe's ear. She returned fire and moved behind a bigger tree.

"If we keep moving out on both sides, one of us might get a better shot at him." Zoe kept her voice low. "What do you think?"

"Worth a try. I'll move first." Jeannie shot at the man and ran to a tree farther to her left.

Zoe did the same on her right. After two more shifts, she'd run out of trees. She hoped Jeannie would get a good angle.

<hr>

VIKTOR PEERED up at the sky. "Spread out and watch for ways you can help. But we must be very careful. The light is beginning to fade. Shadows grow long. I have no way of letting Peter know we are here to help." He shrugged. "He and his friends could mistake us for one of the men sent to kill them."

"We're good at staying in the shadows." The bald man wiped his head before pulling on his balaclava.

"I know you are, my friend."

<hr>

"RAFE." Peter caught his friend as he slid down the side of the house. "You need a doctor."

Rafe waved an arm at him. "I'll be fine. Just need to rest a minute."

"We don't have a minute. They know we're here." Peter pulled Rafe to his feet. "I've got to get you out of here."

Peter stayed close to the house. Supporting Rafe on his left and his gun in his right hand. A few steps. Check the surroundings. Another step. Check. Almost to the corner of the house. He'd have to cross in front of the house to get to Rafe's SUV. The keys.

"Hey buddy, where are your keys?"

"Left pocket."

Great. "Can you get them?"

Rafe dug in his pocket and held them out to Peter. But as Peter reached for them, they dropped to the ground. Peter bent to retrieve them.

"You won't be needing those." The man in the ballcap grinned at Peter as he straightened and aimed his gun right between Peter's eyes.

"Sorry, bro," Rafe murmured.

"Hooah," Peter whispered as Zoe's beautiful face filled his mind.

42

A second man dressed in black appeared out of the shadows behind the man in the ballcap. The spit of a silencer and ballcap man crumbled to the ground. The man in black disappeared into the shadows.

Peter exchanged a glance with Rafe. One of Liska's men? How did he know where to find them?

Rafe's legs gave out.

"Whoa." Peter hauled him to his feet again. "Hospital for you."

As they passed the front of the house, a commotion to their right put Peter on alert. His pulse ratcheted up a notch. Zoe and Jeannie were under fire.

But Rafe needed help.

"I can make it to the SUV on my own," Rafe said. "Take care of the bogey first."

Peter released Rafe and checked his magazine. He bent and started toward the intruder.

"Peter!" Rafe said. "Bogey at three o'clock."

Peter swiveled to fire only to see the bearded man splayed on the porch. Peter jerked around. Rafe leaned against the SUV, right hand holding his gun.

"I owe you. Twice," Peter said.

"Just finish this and get me to a hospital."

Peter turned and pointed his gun at the man behind the rock. "Stop or I'll shoot." He continued forward at a steady pace, gun firm in his hands.

"Just the dude I was hoping to see." The man in the plaid shirt grinned and swung his gun around to aim at Peter.

But he was too slow.

Zoe and Jeannie ran to where Peter stood over the man in the plaid shirt. He wasn't grinning anymore.

"I'm dying. Get me an ambulance." The man held his shoulder. A dark stain appeared beneath him on the grass. "You saw it. He shot me."

"I'm proud of you, Grace," Jeannie said. "I would have killed him."

"I've seen enough death in my life." Peter peered at the man. "Besides, this way you might get some information."

"Good grief." Zoe swung around toward the barn. "We left Madison with a prisoner."

The door opened and Madison stepped out. "Can one of you give me a hand with this guy?"

PETER JOGGED to Rafe's SUV as police cars and ambulances poured into the small amount of open space left in front of Zoe's cabin. His stomach churned as he approached his friend's car. Had Peter waited too long to get him help?

Rafe slumped half inside the SUV on the passenger side, his eyes closed. Peter caught the attention of EMTs. "Need help over here now."

"What happened?" The EMTs headed over.

"He's been shot in the side under his jacket." Peter backed off to give the medical personnel room to work. "His name is Rafe O'Connell."

"Rafe." A young woman paramedic lifted his chin and flashed a light in his eyes. "Look at me. Can you hear me?"

Peter's heartrate slowed when Rafe's eyelids fluttered. The other paramedic inserted an IV into Rafe's arm and left, returning with the ambulance bed.

"Will he be okay?" Zoe touched Peter's shoulder.

"Too soon to tell. He's lost a lot of blood." A vise closed around Peter's heart. Rafe had insisted he help Zoe and Jeannie. But that didn't make him feel any better.

But if he'd taken Rafe to the hospital, Zoe would most likely be dead along with Jeannie and Madison. How would he have felt then?

The attendants lifted Rafe onto the gurney and moved him to the ambulance. One of them motioned to Peter.

"He's asking for you."

Peter strode to Rafe. "What is it, buddy?"

"Set up the meet." Rafe thrust his phone into Peter's hand.

"You concentrate on getting better. Don't worry about—"

Rafe gripped Peter's hand. "Do it." His hand fell to his side, and he closed his eyes.

Peter buried the guilt threatening to paralyze him. He took a deep breath. They were at war, and Rafe had been injured in battle.

The EMTs pushed Rafe into the ambulance and took off, siren and lights blaring.

Lord, let his wounds be minor. Peter surveyed the yard, his eyes landing on Zoe. She'd gone to speak with Madison and Nate. *And protect those left to fight the next battle.*

"Excuse me." Zoe broke away from Madison and Nate to head for Peter.

She recognized the deep lines of worry and exhaustion on his face, and her heart hurt so badly she thought it would break. All she could do was offer a listening ear and a warm hug, but sometimes those were all that was needed. His gaze followed her as she approached.

"Want me to come with you to the hospital?"

"Walk with me by the stream first." Peter took her hand.

When they were away from the cabin and the commotion, he led her into a copse of trees. A breeze rustled the leaves and cooled the exposed skin of her arms and face. Zoe's pulse sped up. Had she misread him? Was he about to tell her he couldn't get involved with anyone?

"Seeing Rafe on the gurney made me realize how much I care about you." Peter stroked her face with his hands, smoothing her hair back off her face. "I'd like you to drop out of this—case."

"Good grief." She stepped back. "You can't be serious. You're asking me to act like some meek little woman and let her man go off to war while she stays at home?"

His shoulders slumped. "I know that's not who you are. It's just—"

"You can't bear the thought of me getting hurt. I get it." She moved closer. "How do you think I feel about you?"

The stench of sweaty man surrounded her, and it never smelled so good. Peter was alive and well. And he cared about her. She threw her arms around his neck.

"I—care about you too, Peter." This wasn't the right time to tell him how she really felt—that care had grown into enduring love.

His arms encircled her and drew her against him. She tilted her head to receive his ardent kiss. Warmth and security flooded through her body. She wanted to remain in his arms forever. But that depended on him.

She broke from their kiss and touched his lips with her finger. "We need to get to the hospital."

Peter pulled his phone from his pocket, looked at the ID, and raised his eyebrows at Zoe.

43

"Liska," Peter spoke into his phone, "I think I owe you one."

"Or two. If you count the man on the porch."

"I thought Rafe took him out."

"No, my friend. Your old pal from the Army was too weak to pull the trigger."

"Then glad you had my back." Peter and Zoe walked toward the cabin. "Where are you?"

"Close."

Peter stopped and scanned the tree line. "Can you see me now?"

"And the lovely Zoe." Liska chuckled. "You should marry the woman. She is a worthy catch as you say in America."

"What would you say where you come from?" Peter listened for road noise or anything that would give Liska's position away. Nothing.

"It is not important. What is important is we continue our talk."

"I'm a little busy right now."

"I understand. But soon. Call me on this number."

The line went dead. Peter pocketed his cell phone and resumed walking.

"Viktor Liska helped you deal with the intruders?" Zoe stopped Peter with a touch of her hand.

"Yes." He pulled her closer. "I'm still not sure why. Or what's so important he needs to tell me. But I want to keep it quiet until I've had a chance to talk with him."

They continued on the path to Zoe's home. By now, all the police vehicles had left except for forensics who were working on the side of the cabin. The fox cubs stuck their noses out from under the porch and peered at them. Peter and Zoe sat on the front steps.

"It's safe," Zoe said. "No more shooting." She held out her hand.

The vixen edged toward Zoe, her belly almost touching the ground. When she got close enough, she wrapped herself in a ball and laid at Zoe's feet. The male remained close but out of reach.

Peter marveled at the scene of tranquility and peace that only a short time ago was one of total chaos. He could stay there forever. But they really needed to check on Rafe.

Peter's phone rang again. "The hospital." He looked at Zoe. Her face reflected the tightening he felt in his chest.

"When are you guys coming to get me?"

"Rafe?" Peter let out a breath.

"You know somebody else in the hospital?"

"The guy I know had one foot in the grave."

"I heal fast."

"We're coming, but no promises to spring you just yet." A furrow creased Peter's brow and he turned to Zoe. "What is it today? People keep hanging up on me."

She chuckled. "We better get over there before Rafe calls a cab."

Peter peered down at his clothes. He should clean up.

"No time for showers, Grace." Zoe hooked her arm through his. "We'll just be smelly together."

"Look." Peter pointed at the hospital entrance as he and Zoe crossed the parking lot.

Rafe sat under the portico on the sidewalk in a wheelchair. A man in blue scrubs stood next to him.

"What are you doing?" Peter said.

"Waiting on my ride."

"I told you." Zoe exchanged an amused look with Peter.

"Told him what?" Rafe squinted up at them.

"I said if we didn't get here soon, you'd call a cab." Zoe crossed her arms. "You don't look so good, boss."

"I tried my best to get him to stay at least one night," the man in blue said. "His wound's been dressed. He's refused blood. Here are his antibiotics and something for pain. He's all yours."

"Thanks, doc," Peter said. "Don't take it personal. He has this thing about hospitals."

Rafe glared at him. "I'm fine. I'll be better once I get back to the rental and can rest. Have you ever been in a hospital? Try to rest in there." He gestured behind him. "Nurses coming and going all the time. Poking and prodding. People moaning and groaning. Doors slamming. Carts rolling down the halls. Might as well have your bed in the middle of a busy intersection."

Peter pressed his lips together to keep from smiling. He glanced at Zoe who rolled her eyes.

"You have a point." Peter faced Rafe. "But you *will* take it easy, or I'll bring you back to the hospital so fast you won't know what hit you."

"Are you going to cancel your cab?" Zoe said.

"Never called one." Rafe threw them a grin.

"Here's your phone." Peter stood next to the burgundy recliner Rafe had brought to the rental house.

"Did you set up the meet with David?"

"I didn't have time. You can set it up yourself." Peter tapped the table next to Rafe's chair. "Only give yourself some time to recoup."

"Yes, mother." Rafe growled.

Peter grinned.

"I want Liska there too." Rafe peered at Peter. "It's time to bring them together."

"We need to find out what Viktor Liska knows first." Peter didn't want any surprises. "I'll call him."

What better time than now. Peter stepped out onto the deck at the back of the house. Light from a half moon reflected off the still water of the lake. No breeze. Intermittent sounds of music drifted from a house across the water. How long had it been since he'd been to a party? Too long.

No time for those thoughts now. He inserted his earbuds and punched in Liska's number. "Let's talk."

"Your old Army buddy, the one from Washington, was the man who hired me to kill Lawrence Merton."

Peter pulled a chair over and sat. "Are you sure?"

"I am good at recognizing voices."

"Do you know why?"

"No," Viktor said. "I never ask. But now he is setting me up as the patsy. Is this what you call it in America?"

"Yes."

"And you as my accomplice. He can divert suspicion from the people behind the killing and can make sure if Merton passed any information to you, it will die with you."

Peter suspected David's involvement, but to hear the proof from Liska was like a blow to the head.

"Peter? Are you still there?" Liska's voice sounded in his ears.

"Yes." He flexed his shoulders. "We're setting up a meet with David, and we want you to be there."

"With pleasure," Viktor said. "It will be dangerous, Peter."

"I'll text you the time and place."

Peter gazed once more at the tranquil waters of Lake Pleasant. He needed to settle past wrongs, make up for his part in Afghanistan. Then maybe with God's help, his life would be his own again, and he'd find peace.

44

"Nate, eat your breakfast. I'm fine." Madison touched her husband's arm. "The EMT's checked me over and everything's great."

"Everything's not great." He laid his spoon on the table. "You've been shot and in a major gun battle in two days."

"But I'm fine." She cut her toast and smiled at him. "I'll be careful. Just like I was yesterday when I stayed in the barn and hid in the loft."

"You mean when you ended up guarding one of the shooters?"

She straightened. "Nate, I don't like being treated like a ... a fragile little lady without a brain." What did men think? When a woman was pregnant, she lost all her common sense?

"You know that's not how I see you." He gulped his coffee and pushed his chair back.

"Then give me some credit." She rose and placed a hand on her stomach. "I'm aware I carry precious cargo, and I'm not going to take any chances."

Nate pulled her into an embrace. "Good. Because you're both precious to me."

"I know." She brushed crumbs from his shirt and raised an

223

eyebrow at him. "But we've had this talk before. I'm not going to live in a cage either."

His arms tightened around her, and a cloud passed so quickly across his deep brown eyes she wasn't sure she'd seen it there at all. She stroked his face and put every ounce of love she had for him into her smile.

"Now go to work. Pleasant Valley counts on you to keep their citizens safe."

"Will—"

She put a finger over his lips. "Rafe, Peter, and Zoe will be next door. Eric will be here with me."

"You stay put," Nate said. "Away from the others. Maybe you'll stay out of trouble."

She kissed him and pushed him out the door. She needed some of Sarah's encouragement and counsel. Madison stopped. She couldn't. Her spirits sagged. Sarah and Ed were in hiding.

And Oscar still fought for his life at the vet's.

Madison's heart ached for her sweet dog. "I think it's porch time, and then make some soup for the guys next door." Surely Nate wouldn't care if they ate lunch together.

MADISON STOPPED STIRRING the soup pot and took a deep breath. The aroma of tomato mixed with onion and other vegetables wafted through the house. She licked her lips. Yum.

The front door opened. "It's me, Mrs. Z," Eric said. "What smells so good?"

"I'm making vegetable soup for lunch."

"An awful big pot for just the two of us."

"No silly. We're taking it over to share with the others." Madison turned to smile at the big man. Her smile faded. "Where's your vest?"

"It's tight." Eric patted his stomach. "Either I got to lose weight or buy a new one."

"Tight or not, please put it on. For my sake if nothing else."

"Sorry." He raised a hand. "I'll get it."

"Thank you," she said. "Then you can carry this pot over to the rental for me."

Madison knew how uncomfortable the bulletproof vests could be, but ever since she'd been shot, she wore hers all day. Even inside. She shuttered. If Nate hadn't been so protective, she wouldn't be here today ... and neither would their child.

PETER GLANCED up from his computer screen at his friend. "Need anything?"

Rafe pushed out of the recliner. "I need to move around."

"Hang on." Peter jumped to his feet.

"I don't need a nursemaid." Rafe glowered at him.

"Don't be so muleheaded."

"I'm not—"

Rafe's left leg gave out and Peter grabbed him before he went down.

"Maybe a little help."

"You're welcome." Peter supported his friend to the kitchen table. "How about some lunch?"

"Do we have anything?"

The door from the deck opened, and Eric and Madison walked in, preceded by a mouth-watering aroma.

"We do now." Peter took the pot from Eric and bent closer to fill his nostrils with the delicious scent.

Zoe appeared from the hallway. "What is that amazing smell?" She yawned. "I was napping until my stomach growled and woke me up."

"It's my homemade tomato vegetable soup." Madison set bowls and spoons on the table. "Some bread to go with it."

When the sounds in the room changed from slurps to spoons

scraping the bottoms of bowls plus a resounding belch from Eric, Peter grabbed his laptop and flipped it open.

"It seems the Washington, D.C. number on the itinerary is listed to Senator Carl Underwood—David's father." Peter stared at the screen in front of him. "Are we looking at the wrong man? Or are they both in on it?"

"The senator could have gotten a set of phones for his staff," Rafe said.

"In that case, it might be anyone who works for Senator Underwood," Zoe said.

"Possible. But my money's on David," Rafe said.

Peter pushed his chair back. His friend's face contorted in pain. "You need to get back in the recliner, buddy."

"I'll help him." Eric scooted his chair back.

"I got this." Rafe braced his hands on the table and prepared to stand. Sweat beaded his forehead as he levered his body into an upright position.

Peter didn't budge. He understood the overpowering desire not only to take care of yourself, but to protect those around you. He'd been there.

Madison took a step forward. Peter motioned for her to stop.

All eyes were on Rafe as he straightened and slowly walked to his chair. Everyone in the room let out a collective breath when their friend and colleague lowered himself once more into his recliner.

"What are you staring at? Never seen a man walk to a chair before?" Rafe growled like an angry bear.

"We were drawing straws on who was going to have to pick you up when—if—you fell, boss," Zoe said.

"Very funny." Rafe ducked his head, but not before Peter caught the shadow of a grin on his face.

"THERE'S the guy and his dog again." Madison pointed to the windows facing the lake. "I don't trust him. Did I tell you he wouldn't let me pet his dog? He said it would upset his training."

"Weird." Zoe scratched her left ear.

"I know. And the dog's collar was really strange."

Peter raised his head. "How so?"

"Thicker than most." Madison shrugged. "With some sort of small canister attachment on the underside."

Peter rose and walked to the window. The man stopped two houses away and bent to pet his dog. It was impossible to see the collar from a distance, but Madison's description set off an itch in his brain. Where had he seen a similar collar before?

"What's his name again?" Peter moved his laptop back to the card table he used for a desk.

"William Smith. But we already vetted him," Rafe said.

"I did this for a living. Remember?" Peter peered at his screen. "He works for the university as an IT guy. Right?"

"Yes."

"A degree in computer science?"

"Trade school." Rafe shook his head. "While Peter's doing his thing, I need updates. Madison, what are you working on?"

"I'm free at the moment."

"Zoe?"

"Hooah." Peter leaned back in his chair. "Our dog walker's IT certification is registered under a William Smith with a different social security number than the one he gave the school."

Rafe stared at him. "You got a job with me anytime. Just say the word."

Peter caught Zoe looking at him. The idea of staying in Pleasant Valley was definitely growing on him.

"I knew that guy meant no good." Madison crossed to the window. "He's gone or I'd—"

"No." Peter moved next to her. "Don't mess with him. If anything else happens to you, I'd never forgive myself."

"You and Eric go back to your house." Rafe pushed to his

feet. "I'll call you if there's anything I need. Rest up for the next battle." He motioned to Peter. "I need to walk around. Loosen my joints."

"I'll leave the pot for now." Madison slid the door to the deck open. "Talk to you later."

"See ya, boss." Eric followed her out.

Rafe made a few circuits with Peter around the living room, kitchen, and eating area. Each time his friend seemed stronger and more sure-footed.

"Do you need help changing the dressing on your wound?"

Rafe shook his head. His phone rang.

"Bring it here, Zoe," Rafe said.

She looked at the screen before handing it to her boss. "It's David Underwood."

"O'Connor." Rafe answered before taking the last few steps to the recliner and easing himself down.

"Not possible." The lines on Rafe's face deepened into furrows. "Change your reservations." His lips pinched into a white line. "Hang on." He pressed mute.

Rafe raised his eyes to Peter. "He wants to meet today. Says he has to leave for D.C. tomorrow morning. Can't change it. Can we get Liska here in time?"

"We can try." Peter pulled his phone from his pocket. "What time?"

"Four-thirty."

"Only a few hours from now," Zoe said.

The three friends glanced at each other. If they didn't set this up now, they may not have another chance.

"Do it." Peter punched Liska's number and walked to the front of the house.

45

"Viktor's on his way." Peter shoved his phone into his back pocket. "Time for a war council."

"I want Eric and a couple others to be here." Rafe turned to Zoe. "Stay with Madison and send Eric over here."

"Won't work." Peter shook his head. "Liska expects Zoe to be here. I'm not sure he'll trust us if she's not."

"Okay." Rafe ran a hand through his hair. "I'll get the others."

"What about Nate?" Zoe said.

"Not until we know for sure David is guilty."

"How will you find out?"

Peter and Rafe shared a knowing look. "That's where Viktor Liska comes in."

"One more thing." Rafe waved Zoe and Peter over. Peter helped him out of the chair and the three friends bowed their heads.

Dear God, help us uncover the truth and uphold justice in a way that brings glory to Your Name. In Jesus name we pray, Amen.

THE DOORBELL RANG and Peter checked the monitor. A man in a gray pin-striped suit with a white shirt and no tie stood on the porch. "It's Liska." Peter opened the door and pulled him inside. "Were you followed?"

"I am crushed you have so little regard for my talents." Liska touched his heart. "One day I will tell you some stories that will make your hair ..." Liska quirked an eyebrow at Peter's buzz cut. "Well, they will impress you."

"No time for stories today. Only the truth."

"Of course." Liska smiled past Peter. "Zoe. I must apologize to her."

"I wouldn't get too close if I were you." Peter watched as Liska approached her from behind.

She turned catching Liska in the ribs with her elbow.

"I'm sorry. I didn't know you were there." Zoe's eyes filled with humor as she slid a kitchen chair in his direction.

Viktor Liska sat and held his side. "No problem, my dear. I deserved it." He coughed and grinned at her. "Are we even?"

"Not yet, but we're getting there."

"Stop fooling around," Rafe barked from the sitting area. "Underwood will be here soon."

"Hey, boss." Two men in jeans and navy RPI T-shirts under their bulletproof vests stepped into the room. "Where do you want us?"

"One at the front door and one at the back." Rafe pointed to the entrances.

Viktor Liska rose and adjusted his jacket. "Where would you like me?"

"First, you need a vest." Peter left the room and soon returned with a flak vest for Liska. "Better to be prepared." Peter held Liska's jacket as the man buckled the vest around his torso. "When David gets here, you'll be in the bedroom. We'll talk to him first and bring you in when we're ready."

"Will I be able to hear your conversation?"

"I'll give you an earpiece." Peter opened a small case on the table.

"A car just entered the subdivision with David and a driver," Rafe said. "We'll talk at the table."

Peter helped his friend cross to the head of the large oak table. A strategic spot. From there, Rafe overlooked the large open room containing the dining table, a sitting area with a gas fireplace, and the card table Peter used for his desk.

The lake glistened in the afternoon sun through floor-to-ceiling windows to his left. Anyone entering off the deck would be visible immediately. A mirror hanging on the far wall reflected down the hall making it possible to have eyes on the front door as well.

"Pat them down when they get here," Rafe said. "Take any weapons and their cell phones."

Viktor caught Peter by the arm and moved in close. "Your friend does not look well."

Peter glanced at Rafe. "He'll be fine. Go on. David's almost here."

Peter positioned himself in the shadows of the unlit kitchen. Better to hear what David would reveal before he saw Peter.

The door opened and Peter heard David's voice, an argument with Rafe's man about being searched. He expected as much. David used to argue with the bartender about being carded. A heaviness settled between his shoulders. He'd trusted David with his life. How could he have been so blind?

"Sit down," Rafe said. "Please."

"What's the problem?" A chair scraped along the wood floor. "I thought you had some news for me about Peter. I came here in good faith and first thing, I get frisked."

"Are you finished?" Rafe's voice chilled the air. "I do have some new information. About a couple of things."

"Is Peter okay?"

"We'll get to Peter in a minute. First, let's talk about the Lawrence Merton's assassination."

"The Merton assassination? Why?"

"Because we have evidence you ordered it."

"Are you out of your mind?"

"Sit down."

"No, I won't sit down."

"Yes, you will."

"Tell your man to take his hands off me." David's voice strident. "Where is my driver?"

"He's being taken care of."

"What evidence could you possibly have?"

"Peter sent the itinerary to you and me. I haven't opened mine. Here it is. You must have been the one to leak it to the newspaper."

"No. I didn't."

"Then how do you explain it?"

"I ... I can't."

Peter entered the room. David sat facing the windows, his head propped in his hands. When he caught sight of Peter, he rose.

"Peter." He took a step in Peter's direction. "It's so good to see you, buddy."

Peter fought to keep his face blank. All those years of friendship blown apart. He looked like David and sounded like David, but he wasn't the man Peter thought he knew, never had been.

"Why did you do it? Never mind." Peter shook his head. "I know why. Money."

"Do what?" David plopped into the chair and stared at Peter.

"The Afghanistan deal, the assassination, killing the kid who lived in my building ..." Peter clenched his fists. "Beating up my grandmother." He needed to get his anger under control.

"Peter, I promise you. I never did any of those things."

David was good. Peter would give him that. His old Army buddy's eyes shimmered with unshed tears.

"You messed up. Your phone number was impressed on the itinerary I found."

"Impossible."

Sweat stains appeared on David's shirt in his armpits, and Peter saw genuine fear in his eyes. No faking. Something wasn't adding up. Time for Liska.

"Viktor, why don't you join us?"

Peter moved to where he could see David's reaction.

"Hello, Mr. Underwood." Viktor Liska gave David a big smile. "Finally, we meet in person."

"Do I know you?"

No recognition showed in David's face. Either he was one of the best liars Peter had ever seen, or ...

"You hired me to kill Lawrence Merton."

"No." David jumped up. "I've never seen you before in my life."

"But we spoke on the phone, and I never forget a voice." Liska tapped his ear.

David collapsed into the chair. He slumped over the table, eyes glazed. Peter and Liska took seats across from him. When David raised his head, defeat transformed his face into a man older than his years. And Peter knew. They had won.

"You said you found my phone number on the itinerary. May I see it?" David whispered.

"I don't see why not." Peter caught Zoe's eye.

She retrieved a copy of the phone number from a folder.

As David read it, his chin quivered.

"This is my father's cell phone number." He closed his eyes for a moment.

"But I heard your voice." Viktor leaned across the table. "I am certain."

"We sound alike on the phone." David gave Rafe a pleading look. "If you'll give me my cell phone, I'll prove it."

Rafe motioned for his guy to get David's phone. Once in hand, David tapped the screen a few times.

"This is a message Dad left me just before I came here." David touched the screen, and a voice filled the room.

Peter and Rafe turned to Viktor, who nodded yes. David Underwood and the man who left the message, his father, Senator Carl Underwood, did indeed sound alike on the phone.

"I knew he was into something, but I still can't believe it involved killing innocent people." Tears filled David's eyes.

"Unless you were in on it with your dad and you took care of the murders," Rafe said.

"I saw enough violence and death in the Army." David's eyes had a haunted look. "I've struggled with those memories ever since."

But if David wasn't in league with his father, how had Carl seen the itinerary? Realization hit Peter. Unless Carl created it. Viktor said he'd never seen it before.

"Do you know this guy?" Rafe showed David a picture on his phone of William Smith.

"I knew him in the Army. He trained dogs to deliver—"

"Incendiary devices." Peter thumped the table. "I knew Madison's description of the dog's collar sounded familiar."

"—into enemy territory." David peered at Peter. "He works for Dad now. Why do you ask?"

"Check the perimeter," Rafe barked to his man standing by the back door.

Rafe's man pulled the sliding door opened and stepped onto the deck, closing the door behind him.

"Has Smith been here?" David's eyes widened.

"Does your dad know about our meeting?" Rafe said.

"No, but—"

"Boss." Rafe's man yanked the door open. "Under the deck. We need to—"

The blast sent Rafe's man hurtling into the room.

46

Madison felt the blast a millisecond before she heard it. Shockwaves traveled through the ground, shaking the walls in her lab. She grabbed a bottle of sulfuric acid sitting near the edge of the lab table and placed it in the sink. Last thing she needed was a spill right now.

Gloves off and apron thrown over a stool, she scooped up the itinerary from Peter, the note and arrows from Zoe, her files on the case, and shoved them into her fireproof safe. She headed for the door, her heart pounding in her ears. Another sound reached her. One she knew too well.

"Mrs. Z," Eric met her at the bottom of the stairs, "the rental's on fire."

"Where are Rafe, Peter, and Zoe?" Madison grappled with the locks on the door to the outside. Stiff from disuse, it took both hands to make them yield.

"They had a meeting." Eric blocked Madison from stepping outside.

"What meeting? Why wasn't I invited?" Her jaw tightened. Pregnancy was not a valid reason to keep her out of a meeting, and she would make sure Rafe knew how she felt. Just as soon as she made sure he was okay.

"Mrs. Z. Please." Eric stuck his head out and scanned the area.

"Sorry. I get a little crazy."

"Let's go."

Hungry flames devoured the deck to the rental home before her. The fire was like a wild animal seeming to have a cunning all its own. For a moment, she was back in the cabin in southern Indiana—the animal surrounding her and smoke filling her lungs.

"We need to wet your house down so the fire doesn't spread." Eric sprinted to where the garden hose lay curled neatly under the deck. He screwed the nozzle on and opened the spigot as wide as it would go.

"I'll take this one. You get the one in front." She yanked the hose into position and sprayed water on the cedar siding— turning her back on the beast next door. She touched her necklace.

PETER SHOT TO HIS FEET. Zoe and Viktor rushed to Rafe's fallen man inside the door. Rafe pushed himself erect at the head of the table while David remained seated, the color drained from his face.

"Get moving, soldier." Peter barked in David's direction.

He blinked and rose.

"Help Rafe get out of here."

"I don't need—" Rafe closed his mouth at a look from Peter.

Good. He'd understood. Rafe was to keep an eye on David. While Peter kept track of Viktor. Couldn't have either of them wandering off in the confusion.

Rafe's man groaned and pushed to his feet. Zoe and Viktor supported him as smoke swirled through the room. Peter glanced at the gas fireplace. They needed to hurry.

"Double time, people." Peter led the way to the front door.

Rafe's front door man laid on the driveway with David's driver standing over him.

"What's going on?" Peter stepped onto the porch.

A bullet hit the doorframe next to his head. Milliseconds later, the sound reverberated off the houses. Peter reversed direction, slamming the door behind him.

"What now?" Liska said.

"The garage." Peter herded them back across the smoke-filled room to the kitchen. "Pull your shirts over your nose and mouth."

Once inside the two-car garage, Peter stuffed rags along the bottom edge of the door.

"We'll have to go through this window." Peter shoved a box out of the way. It wouldn't be easy. Small opening.

"If we can break the seal, we can remove the window completely." David rummaged through a toolbox. "Here we go." He held up a couple of hammers and large screwdrivers.

"Show me what to do," Peter said.

Within minutes, the window frame was off.

"Now we need brute force. Push on the edges, not the glass, and it should pop out," David said.

With a screech, the window tumbled to the ground below.

"Good job." Peter clapped David on the shoulder. "I'll go first."

Outside, thick smoke caused them to cough. Peter's first reaction was to get them away from the fire raging to their right, but common sense told him there was more than one shooter.

"Stay as close to the smoke as you can." Peter said. "Spread out and keep low."

"Where are we headed?"

"Sarah and Ed's house," Rafe said.

As they started across the yard, a shot rang out. Rafe stumbled and David caught him. Peter's stomach lurched.

Another shot echoed off the lake. David spun away from

Rafe and dropped to the ground. Rafe's man ran toward his fallen boss. A third shot and the man fell.

Out of the corner of his eye, Peter caught a figure running his way.

MADISON TRAINED a stream of water on her house. If the fire jumped to her home, her laboratory could explode, taking everything with it.

But what about the rental? It ran on natural gas. The meter hung on the back of the house with a shut-off valve. Could she get to it?

She turned the hose on herself, shivering as water doused her from head to toe. She took off across the yard.

A loud crack echoed off the lake.

Gunfire?

Her steps faltered. Rafe and another man lay prone on the grass. Should she offer assistance or complete her mission? Shut off the gas—or they would all die in the explosion.

As she neared the back wall of the house, scorching heat from the fire quickly evaporated her water barrier and singed her hair. She reached for the metal shut-off valve. Fiery hot pain seared her palm and shot up her arm. Whipping off her flannel shirt, she wrapped her hand and closed the valve.

Shivering in only her T-shirt, Madison ran to Rafe and the other man. She knelt and felt for a pulse in each. Both alive, but they needed help. Where were Peter and Zoe?

"GET DOWN." Peter called to Madison, but his words drowned in the roar of the fire.

Eric ran between the houses. Peter waved him over, motioning for him to stay low.

"I lost Mrs. Z." Eric crouched by Peter. "She was watering her house. Then I heard a shot and she disappeared."

"She's up there." Peter lifted his chin in her direction. A thin veil of smoke surrounded her and two other figures. A lump formed in Peter's throat. "Rafe and David Underwood have been shot."

Four people appeared from around the side of the rental house. David's driver held a gun to Zoe's side, her hands bound in front of her. Another man prodded Viktor along in the same manner. Peter pushed to his feet. Every muscle tensed.

"Peter, my friend, it seems David was telling the truth." Viktor glanced at David's driver. "But there was a fox in the hen house."

"Shut up." The man gave Viktor a push, and he stumbled before regaining his balance.

"Too bad you found out too late to tell David you believe him." A voice came from behind Peter. William Smith faced Peter but kept his distance. "You're a hard man to find. By the time I realized you were living here, you'd gone to stay with the woman at her cabin. We had to change our plans."

"That didn't work out so well. Did it?" Peter smirked.

"It did exactly what we wanted it to do." Smith grinned back. "It sent you back here. Now we have you all together in one nice, neat bundle."

"How do you propose to make our deaths appear believable?"

"The fire of course. A gas explosion wipes you all out in one big boom."

"But what about Rafe and David? Forensics is good these days. They'll still show signs of being shot."

"We'll let the authorities figure that one out." Smith waved his gun at Peter. "Time to get you all back into the house."

"The neighbor's will have called the fire department. The trucks should be here any minute."

"There's been an unfortunate accident blocking the road into your subdivision. It's going to take a while for them to get through." Smith jabbed Peter in the ribs with his automatic pistol. "Stop stalling."

Anger rolled through Peter. He grabbed the barrel of the gun and twisted it up and away. It exploded next to his ear. Smith released his grip, and the gun flew several feet away. He struck Peter in the neck with the side of his hand before pulling a knife from his belt.

With a yell, Eric ran at Smith. Smith pivoted and thrust his arm at the charging man.

"No!" Peter watched Eric crash to his knees, hands clasping his abdomen. Blood oozed from between his fingers.

Peter dove for Smith's gun, rolled, and fired. His shot went wide.

47

Madison kneeled by Rafe. Her heart lurched as Zoe and Viktor Liska came into sight, their hands tied. Someone touched her arm, and she let out a cry. Rafe. She bent closer.

"Get my gun. I can't move fast enough to help, but you can."

Madison's hands trembled. Could she? Now that she was being treated as a competent woman and not some delicate little lady, doubts raged against her.

She grabbed the cross at her neck and glanced at the men holding Zoe and Liska. They hadn't noticed her. The snap and snarl of the flames nearby made it impossible for her to hear what was being said, but it also covered sounds from her as well.

The Lord is my strength and my shield. My heart trusts in Him.

She crept along the house, staying at the edge of the smoke. Almost there.

PETER NEEDED HER HELP. Zoe took a step in his direction only to be yanked back like a dog on a chain. Blood pounded in her ears. With a guttural roar, Zoe threw herself backwards. She landed on David's driver in a tangle of arms and legs. She jabbed

241

her captor in the face with her elbow. The crunch of bone on bone.

Zoe rolled to her right, grabbed his wrist with her hands, and applied pressure. His grip loosened.

The gun fell to the grass.

She scrambled to her knees.

The pistol lay within reach.

A kick to her ribs.

She sprawled across the ground once more. He stretched toward the pistol. A foot stomped on his hand.

"I wouldn't if I were you." A familiar voice.

Zoe raised her eyes. Madison aimed a Glock at the head of David's driver.

Another man charged around the corner of the house, gun raised. He fired at Viktor.

AT THE SOUND of a commotion next to him, Viktor inched away from the man holding him. As he'd hoped, the man was too distracted to notice. The pressure from the gun in his side lessened.

Viktor pivoted and brought his bound hands down on the man's wrist, and the weapon fell from his captor's numb fingers. Quick to react, the man swung at Viktor.

Viktor dodged the blow and grinned. He moved into the man. With a swift motion, he butted the man's head with his. A brief frown crossed the man's brow. Had Viktor misjudged the spot? If so ...

The man's eyes rolled back in his head, and he collapsed. Viktor sighed. He had not lost his abilities. Now to help the lovely Zoe. His smile broadened. It seemed she did not need his help after all.

Something slammed into him spinning him like a skater on ice. He crumbled to the ground. Searing pain.

PETER'S STOMACH knotted as he caught sight of the new bogey. How many more were out there?

David's driver got to his feet and retrieved his weapon. He motioned Zoe and Madison down the yard closer to Peter and William Smith. As Zoe came within reach, Smith pulled her to him and put his knife to her throat.

"Put the gun down, Grace." Smith pricked Zoe under the chin. A bright red tear ran down her neck.

"Don't, Peter." Zoe's eyes caught his in a fierce stare. "We're going to die anyway."

Smith forced her closer. "Look at her, Peter. Her death won't be a quick one."

But Peter knew something Smith didn't. He didn't notice the motion behind him as the police silently moved in and took over. Peter smiled and laid the gun on the ground.

"But *your* death will be very quick if you don't put the knife down." Nate placed his gun against Smith's head.

The calvary had arrived. Hooah. Firetrucks and ambulances. Sirens never sounded so good.

Peter closed the distance to Zoe in two strides. He enfolded her in his arms, relief surging through him.

Until his gaze fell on their fallen comrades. Rafe leaned on a policeman.But attendants pushed David and Viktor across the uneven lawn toward waiting ambulances and carried Rafe's man away in a body bag. EMTs performed CPR on Eric. Peter took Zoe's hand and headed for Rafe.

"Where were you hit?" Zoe said.

"Wasn't. My leg gave out." Rafe shifted his weight. "Couldn't get back to my feet." The dark cloud of a scowl crossed his face. "Weak and useless. I should have stayed in the hospital."

"No time for 'should haves'," Peter said. "We need to assess our losses and make a plan."

Madison and Nate approached with Madison tucked under her husband's arm.

"It sure was good to see you." Peter shook Nate's hand.

"When the calls started coming in from our neighbors about the fire and gunshots ..." Nate kissed Madison on the head. "I knew I needed to get here pronto."

"You know if it weren't for Madison, I'd probably be dead," Zoe said.

"I heard." Nate smoothed a wisp of hair off his wife's face.

Madison fixed him with something just short of a glare.

"She's pretty amazing." Nate hugged her to him, and she rewarded him with a smile.

"Enough mush. I need to sit down." Rafe grumbled. "Help me to Aunt Sarah's house."

Nate signaled a couple of men to follow. "I'll need full accounts from each of you."

Peter stopped. "There were two shooters. One in the woods out front, and one across the lake."

Nate spoke to one of the officers and returned his attention to Peter. "Anything else?"

"Not right now."

Peter's thoughts kept returning to David and Viktor. One an old friend who Peter thought had betrayed his trust, and another who started as an enemy, but ended as a trusted ally. Both willing to risk their lives to see a man put behind bars—one motivated by justice and one by revenge. If they didn't make it, they would have given their lives for nothing. The case against Senator Carl Underwood would fall apart. His phone number on the itinerary could be argued away as an attempt to frame him. They needed more.

At Sarah's house, Peter got Rafe settled and found a spot at the kitchen table for Nate and his officer to take their statements. Rafe's cell phone binged with a text.

"Peter." Rafe waved him over, his blue eyes snapping with

renewed energy. "My man found something on the memory stick from Merton."

Peter took the phone from his friend. The corners of his mouth tugged up into a wide grin. This could be it. The nail in Senator Carl Underwood's coffin. Peter read through the analysis again. He found no flaws in the reasoning. The evidence clearly showed Underwood as the instigator of the Afghanistan fraud and the one who profited most from its inception.

They only needed to prove he was willing to kill to keep his part in the enterprise secret. That's where Viktor came in—and David.

If they lived.

Viktor, eyes shut, willed his right hand to move. No use. Start with the fingers. First one. Yes. An alarm sounded very close. Was he dreaming? Why couldn't he lift his arm?

"He's waking up. Get the doctor."

Doctor? He had been ice skating on the pond by his house in Pilsen. He spun too fast, fell, and hit his head. No, that wasn't it.

"Mr. Liska. I'm Doctor Innes. Can you open your eyes?"

A man's voice. Viktor concentrated on the task. His eyelids lifted, and he squinted into a bearded face with wire-rimmed glasses.

"Where am I?" Viktor said in Czech.

"I'm sorry. I only speak English." The doctor smiled at him. "You're in Pleasant Valley Hospital. You've been shot in the head."

The meeting, the fire, the fight—all played through his mind in a rush like a movie on fast forward. His pulse sped up, and the machine next to him sounded off again.

"Please. Try to stay calm." The doctor laid a hand on his shoulder. "We're considering how to remove the bullet. For now, you need to remain as still as possible."

"I must speak to Peter Grace." Viktor pinned the doctor with his eyes. "It is a matter of extreme urgency."

PETER JOINED Nate at Sarah and Ed's table. "Are you about done? We need to get to the hospital."

"We just finished." Nate closed his notebook. "I'm on my way over there too. Want a ride?"

"I don't know how long Zoe and I will stay," Peter said.

"Then I'll ride with you," Nate said. "I've got a few things I need to discuss with you."

Madison sat in a chair by Rafe. "I'll stay here. Let me know how Eric and the others are."

"I'm leaving an officer here with you two." Nate raised a hand. "No arguments." He kissed Madison on top of her head.

Madison looked at her phone. She raised her fingers to her cross. "It's the vet calling."

"Answer it, sweetheart." Nate laid a hand on her shoulder.

"What if ..." Tears shimmered in her eyes.

Peter and Zoe moved to her side. A weight pressed on Peter's chest. Madison couldn't take it if anything happened to Oscar. He glanced at Nate. Nate would have a hard time too.

"Do you want me to talk to them?" Zoe said.

"No." Madison straightened and threw Zoe a brief smile. "He's my puppy. Good or bad, I need to hear the results myself."

The clouds dissolved from Madison's face, and the load lifted from Peter's heart.

"Oscar's coming home." Madison's smile lit up the room. "He's healed." She jumped up and grabbed her husband around the neck.

Peter reached for Zoe's hand and squeezed it gently. They needed some good news. The Lord alone knew what they would hear at the hospital.

Peter glanced in his rearview mirror at Nate. "What did you want to discuss?"

"What's your plan for going after Senator Underwood?"

"If David is able, we hope he can get his dad to say something implicating himself on a recorded phone call."

"Then what? If he gets wind of what's going on ..." Nate shrugged. "You're here and he's in D.C. How do you catch him?"

"You have a suggestion?" Zoe said.

"Detective Bernadette Santo's fiancé, FBI agent Dr. Daniel O'Leary. He'll have connections in Washington, men who could be ready to pounce when you say the word."

"Of course." Zoe tapped her temple with her fingers. "Daniel."

"You know him?" Peter flipped a look her way.

"We were on a case together last year. He's a good guy."

"Let's get him over here."

Zoe stared out the front window, a big grin on her face. What was she thinking about?

"So, how well did you know this Daniel guy?" Peter said low enough he hoped Nate couldn't hear.

"Oh, Peter." Zoe chuckled and shook her head.

"We're here." Nate inclined his head out the window at a sprawling two-story building with a large portico in the middle.

At the information desk, the three split up with Peter and Zoe headed for Eric, and Nate for Liska. As Peter and Zoe worked their way toward Eric's room, the big man's face, eyes wide with shock, played through Peter's mind once again. *Please God, spare him.*

"He's still in recovery." The nurse checked her computer. "It may be some time. Do you want me to text you when he's back in his room?"

"Please." Peter gave her his number. The knot formed in his

stomach again. How many would have to die before this was all over?

Zoe touched his hand. "David or Viktor?"

Peter felt the familiar vibration in his pocket. He pulled out his phone. "Grace."

"Liska wants to talk to you. Now." Urgency clipped Nate's words. "He's bad."

"Be right there." Peter grabbed Zoe's hand and jogged through the halls of the hospital.

At Viktor's door, Peter paused. He bowed his head briefly and went in. A hollow man lay in the bed—nothing like the vibrant Czech Peter had come to know. Only the eyes were the same. Dark and piercing.

"Come closer, my friend," Viktor whispered.

Peter moved next to him.

"I wish to make a video statement ..." Viktor took in a deep breath. "Before they operate." Another breath. "Will it be admissible in your courts?"

Peter cut his eyes to Nate who shrugged. "I won't lie to you. I'm not sure, but we've got nothing to lose."

"My exact thoughts." Viktor closed his eyes. "Set it up please. Hurry, Peter."

"I'll call in one of our videographers." Nate stepped into the hall.

"I'm going to check on David," Zoe said. "I'll call you."

Peter settled into the chair next to Viktor's bed. He closed his eyes and let the gentle whirring of the machines monitoring Liska's vital signs lull him.

"Peter," Viktor said in a low voice.

He peered at the man in the bed. Had Viktor spoken or—

"Do you think your God would forgive me for all the lives I've taken?" Liska spoke without opening his eyes.

"Yes. If you're really sorry for what you've done and repent." Peter laid his hand on Viktor's. "God's been there you're whole life. Waiting for you, Viktor."

"He is truly a great God if He can forgive a man like myself." A tear traced the furrows in the assassin's cheek.

What greater sin did this man have than Peter? How many deaths came about from his intel in the Army? Some of them had to be collateral damage—innocents killed along with bad guys.

And if he'd closed his eyes to the Afghanistan fraud in the beginning when he'd first learned of it, none of this would have happened. He'd still be in the Army. Lawrence Merton and the kid in his apartment building would still be alive. Eric wouldn't be fighting for his life. David Underwood and Viktor—

He pinched the bridge of his nose. Flawed thinking. Lawrence Merton could have died from cancer and the kid across the landing was headed for jail or worse. Eric, David, and Viktor—well, who knows?

The truth was he wouldn't have reacted any other way—and God's in control.

"My guy's on his way." Nate came through the door, head down. "Also, I called Daniel and he's coming over." He raised his head. "Is everything okay?"

"Yeah." Peter scrubbed his hands down his face. "Just tired. Viktor's resting."

His phone vibrated. A text. Eric was out of surgery. Peter pressed in Zoe's number.

49

———

Zoe showed her credentials to the policeman outside David's room. The door stood ajar, and the sound of muffled voices reached her in the quiet hallway.

"Who's in there?" She inclined her head toward the door.

"His doctor." The officer handed her ID back. "You'll need to—"

"Great." Zoe pulled the door open.

"Who are you?"

A clean-shaven man in black pants, blue dress shirt, and tie stood next to David's bed. A stethoscope hung from his neck, and displeasure twisted what was probably a very handsome face.

"I'm a private investigator." Zoe flashed her ID. "Who are you?"

"Mr. Underwood's doctor, and this is my hospital." He replaced the stethoscope in his ears. "You'll have to wait outside until I'm finished."

Zoe glanced at the other person in the room, a nurse with a clipboard. She shrugged in a sorry-nothing-I-can-do gesture. Zoe winked at her and pulled up a chair. Her phone buzzed with a text. Eric was out of surgery.

If she left David's room now, she would miss her chance to

253

ask questions about his condition. And face it, she'd hate to lose her little battle of wills with the arrogant doc.

But Eric may need a friend about now. She pushed to her feet.

"We repaired Mr. Underwood's shoulder." The doctor straightened. "His blood loss was minimal. He should be fine in a day or two to be released for rehab." He gave a brisk nod to the nurse, brushed past Zoe, and out the door.

The nurse stopped in front of her and held up her fist for a bump.

Zoe stepped to David's bed. He was resting peacefully. Time to see about Eric. Why couldn't their rooms all be on the same hall? For a small hospital, it still managed to be hard to navigate. Hospital architects must take a special class on building mazes.

After one wrong turn, she found Eric's room. Another officer at another door and another doctor inside the room. Only this time he welcomed her in.

"Eric, a friend is here to see you." The bearded man patted his patient's arm.

"Good to see you, buddy." Zoe touched his hand.

Eric gave her a weak smile.

"He's a warrior, this one," the doctor said. "It will take a while, but he should recover to fight another day."

Tears flooded Zoe's eyes. *Thank You, Jesus.*

"I'll leave you two alone."

Zoe caught the doctor at the door. "Tell me what you didn't want to say in front of him."

"Lots of repair." The bearded man glanced back into the room. "We had to take his spleen and part of his liver. The knife just missed his left lung." He frowned at Zoe. "Why wasn't he wearing a vest?"

"He was, but he'd unbuckled it. His assailant was able to thrust the knife up under the vest."

The doctor shook his head. "He's lucky to be alive."

Zoe touched her tattoo. Not lucky. Protected and sheltered.

THOUGHTS OF ERIC kept Peter on his feet pacing Viktor's hospital room. Why hadn't Zoe reported back yet?

"The videographer is here." Nate looked up from his phone. "Get Zoe."

Peter punched her number. "We're ready. Come to Viktor's room."

The door swung open, and Peter cut his circuit short to pivot in that direction. A man lugging two heavy bags pushed through the door.

"Where do you want me?"

Nate sprung to his feet. "Let me help."

Zoe poked her head in, and Peter motioned her to the windows.

"How's Eric?"

"I was about to call you." She smiled at him. "It was a rough surgery, but he's good."

"David?"

"Him too." She rested her hip against the windowsill and gazed at Viktor. "How's he doing?"

"He's losing ground." His throat tightened around his words.

Nate waved them over. "We're all set. Let's get started. I'll conduct the interview. We'll begin with introductions of all the people present in the room along with their credentials."

PETER HELPED the videographer pack up his equipment. "Thanks for helping out. You okay getting to your car?"

The man nodded and left the room.

"Thanks, Nate. I owe you." Peter stuck out his hand.

"My pleasure and my duty." Nate grabbed his jacket from the chair. "We'll get this processed and have it ready when you are."

The door closed and Peter turned to see Zoe sitting next to

Viktor, her beautiful face damp from crying. He pulled a chair close on the other side of the bed.

"Thank you, Peter." Viktor's voice no louder than a whisper.

"Thank *you*, my friend," Peter said.

A smile spread across the man's face.

The alarms sounded next to his bed.

PETER WALKED to the small sitting area at the end of the hospital hall. He pulled his phone from his pocket.

"Rafe." Peter rubbed his forehead. "Viktor's heart stopped. They're working on him now."

"I'm sorry, Peter. This is the tough part of war—and life."

"Yeah."

"Keep me posted and let me know what I can do."

"I will." Peter pushed end.

Zoe sat beside him and slid her hand into his.

The doctor appeared in front of them. "I'm sorry. We did our best."

Peter rose and shook his hand. "Thank you." A lump formed in his throat. "I know you did."

Zoe wrapped him in her arms, and he buried his face against her neck. Another death. Was it worth it? To expose the schemes of a greedy senator?

How many brothers-in-arms had he seen die in battle? He'd shoved his grief to one side and carried on because he had to. But that was war.

Rafe would say this was a war too, a war for justice. Should Peter treat Viktor's death as a fallen comrade and push on with their plan? If he didn't, Viktor's endurance long enough to make his video statement was for nothing. But if he gave the senator the flash drive, he could end the war and prevent any future casualties.

Peter leaned back and framed Zoe's face with his hands. "What should I do? Push on or stop fighting?"

"Oh, Peter." She took his hands in hers. "You already know the answer. And I'll be with you to the end."

How had he gotten through life without her? She completed him.

"Love is not a big enough word for what I feel for you," Peter whispered.

"I know." Her mouth covered his in a kiss. After a moment, she drew back. "We'll revisit this later when we have time." She touched her lips. "I've been thinking. Let's give the senator the flash drive."

But he thought—

"At least, let him *think* we are." Sparks flashed in her violet eyes.

50

Peter finished his coffee and held the door for Zoe. Morning light flooded into David Underwood's hospital room. Nate and another man worked with recording equipment next to the bed.

"How're you feeling?" Peter smiled at his friend.

"Nervous."

"Remember David," Peter said, "the senator has to retrieve the drive himself. Tell him whatever you have to, but we need him to accept the package."

David nodded.

An ache throbbed in Peter's chest. He'd asked his friend to betray his father. An action that, no matter the reason, took something away from everyone involved.

"David, I ... thank you." Peter clasped his hand briefly.

"He did some bad things, Peter." David turned haunted eyes on Peter. "And I'm not stupid. The bullet that hit my shoulder was meant for me. My father tried to kill me." He looked at his phone. "I hope I can hold it together and convince him of what you want me to say."

"You'll do fine." Peter squeezed his good shoulder. "Ready?"

"Let's do this."

Peter scanned the room. Zoe sat in a far corner. Nate and his technician stood next to the bedside table. At a nod from Peter, David pressed in a number on his phone and the technician started recording.

"Dad," David said. "I've been shot. I'm in the hospital."

"What happened? How bad is it?"

The Senator's voice sounded loud and clear.

"I was at a meeting when the house caught fire. When we ran out, we were ambushed. I got shot in the shoulder. I need surgery but should be okay."

"David, how terrible." The sound of shuffling paper. "What kind of meeting were you at?"

"I tracked down Peter Grace. I'd gone to meet with him and some people he knows."

"Peter Grace? Your old Army friend who's messed up in the Merton assassination?"

"Yes, but Dad, turns out he had nothing to do with it. But he thought I was behind it."

Silence.

"Are you there?" David said.

"Yes, yes. I lost you for a minute. Did you say Grace thought you ordered the Merton assassination?"

"Yes. I was able to convince him it wasn't me. Thankfully." David glanced at Peter. "But we figured out someone in the government has to be. That's where you come in."

"Me?"

The pitch of the senator's voice changed. Peter caught Nate's eye.

"Yes. Peter has evidence of fraud going on in Afghanistan having to do with transport companies. Lawrence Merton sent it to him just before he was killed. We're sure that's why those guys came after us the other day."

"Really? Hang on a second." The senator muted his phone for a moment. "I'm back. So how can I help?"

"Peter has given the evidence to me, but he insists I give it to you in person. No go-betweens because of the sensitive nature of its contents." David paused for a breath. "I'd like you to pick it up. You can get to work on finding who's behind all this while I'm still recuperating. The sooner we nail this guy, the better. And I told Peter you're just the man for the job."

"I appreciate your confidence, son. I'll catch the next flight out," the senator said. "Take care of yourself and the memory stick."

David pushed *end* and gave Peter a sad look. "I never told him it was a memory stick."

"YOUR FATHER'S plane touched down fifteen minutes ago." Peter stood over David's bed. "Here's the flash drive. It's not the real thing but it's good enough to fool him if he should bring a computer to check it out. The play may not get that far."

David's hand trembled as he took the memory stick from Peter.

"It's almost over. I'll have Zoe come in dressed as a nurse," Peter said. "Keep the conversation going as she takes your pulse and moves around the room. That way your dad will be less inclined to notice her."

"What if he has a bodyguard?" A light sheen of perspiration shone on David's forehead.

"There's still an officer at your door. He'll make him stay outside."

"Where will you be?"

"Nate and I will be next door. Along with Daniel, our FBI friend." Peter pointed to the wall behind the bed. "We'll be able to hear and see everything happening in here. If you feel like you need us for any reason, just say the word."

PETER GREETED NATE AND DANIEL. "I've got monitors set up for us to watch and hear what goes on next door, and everything will be recorded."

"Good." Daniel scanned the equipment. "You've thought of everything. When do we expect the senator?"

"Anytime. In fact ..." Peter's chest tightened as he watched the camera show the senator push through the door into David's hospital room. Would his friend be able to maintain his cool?

"Son. How are you?" Senator Carl Underwood covered the distance to David's hospital bed in three strides.

Peter switched views to a different camera to get a better view of the senator's face. Nate and Daniel took a seat before the other two screens.

"I'm okay," David said. "You got here quickly."

"You said you needed me." The senator flashed his son a smile.

"I do. Sit down."

"Okay."

An adjustment to the camera angle and the senator's face was once more in view.

"What's on your mind? I thought we'd already done our talking."

"Not quite." David's voice chilled the air.

"What's going on, David?"

"I know you're behind the Afghanistan fraud, Lawrence Merton's assassination, the bomb, and the attempt on my life."

"You're talking nonsense." Carl Underwood jumped to his feet.

"No, Dad. I've seen the evidence."

"What evidence? The memory stick you're holding? You said you hadn't seen what was on it."

"I haven't. Sit down, Dad."

The senator dragged the chair back and sat once more.

"What else leads you to believe I could do such things?"

"An imprint of your phone number on the itinerary left by one of your bozos along with the testimony of the assassin himself. He recognized your voice. At first, they thought it was me because we sound alike on the phone. That's when I knew for certain."

"*The assassin.*" *Carl Underwood snorted.* "*He's dead. He won't be giving either of us any problems anymore.*"

"*No. He's not. The police put out misinformation. They've taken him into protective custody.*"

Fear skirted across Carl Underwood's features.

"*Impossible.*"

"*It's not. And there's more.*" *David paused.* "*Your guy, the one who calls himself William Smith? He's talking—telling the police all he knows.*"

The senator passed a shaky hand over his brow. He stared at his son.

"*Let me have the flash drive. My lawyers can take care of the rest.*"

"*So, you are guilty.*" *A statement, not a question from David.*

Peter pulled the camera view back to see more of the senator and the bed on his monitor.

"*What if I am?*" *The senator's voice rose.* "*You and your mother didn't seem to mind the money I was making when you were spending it.*"

"*And the assassination? All the other people hurt or killed to cover up your Afghanistan scheme?*"

"*Don't you listen to the news?*" *Indignant now.* "*I'm being talked about as a candidate for vice president. I couldn't let this come out.*"

"*You were willing to sacrifice your own son for the vice-presidency?*"

"*My orders were to wing you. Which they did,*" *the senator said.* "*Now I wish I'd told them to go for the kill shot.*"

"*Too late now.*"

The senator pulled a gun from his pocket and pointed it at David.

"*One advantage to being a U.S. Senator. You never have to go through—*"

Nurse Zoe entered David's room, voice muffled. "*Good afternoon Mr.—*"

51

Peter tensed and pulled the view back to include more of the room.

"We need to get in there." Nate headed for the door.

Daniel pushed his chair back. "We've got all we need."

"Wait. Give Zoe a chance to de-escalate." Peter's leg bounced as he monitored the scene in the room next door. "We don't need any more people hurt or dead."

The senator swung his gun around at Zoe.

"No—"

"Whoa. I'm one of the good guys." Zoe chuckled. "You can put that thing away. Only here to take his vitals, not his life." She waggled her clipboard.

The senator dropped his arm to his side but kept his gun in his hand.

She peered at the machines next to David's bed and made some notes.

"The way you're guarded, either you're a really bad guy, or a really important person." She smiled at David. "I think you must be important with such a handsome face."

She moved around the end of bed toward the senator.

"Excuse me. I need to get to this side now."

She squeezed past him.

"Either way, rest assured we at the hospital will do our very best to mend your shoulder and get you feeling better."

She took David's pulse and gave him a wink.

"That's my girl," Peter said under his breath.

"What did you say?" Nate said.

"Watch and learn. She's about to pull the same maneuver she pulled on Viktor at the rental."

"Everything looks good for now." Zoe stepped back. Right on the senator's toe.

"Ouch."

"I'm so sorry." Zoe turned.

An elbow to his ribs, and he bent over. She smacked him in the face with her clipboard. His gun skittered across the floor. A push and he's in the chair.

Beauty in motion. Peter sighed.

"Let me get that for you." Zoe strode over to where his pistol lay. She picked it up by the barrel, preserving the senator's prints, and placed it on the table. "It's safe to come in now, guys." She withdrew her revolver from inside the waistband of her baggy scrubs. "Nice to finally meet you, Senator Underwood."

Nate and Daniel headed for the room next door. Peter continued to record.

"Senator Carl Underwood, please stand," Nate said.

"That crazy nurse attacked me." The senator jabbed a finger at Zoe. "Tell them, David."

David turned away from his father.

"You have the right to remain silent ..." Nate tugged the senator's arms behind his back and continued reading him his rights. "Do you understand these rights as I have told them to you?"

"Of course, but—"

"Officer, take the senator to a holding cell."

"This is an outrage."

"Stop." David roared at his father. "They've recorded and videoed everything, Dad."

Senator Underwood turned to gape at his son in disbelief. "You set me up."

"Yes."

Peter's chest hurt at the pain in David's one word answer.

"Get him out of here," Nate said.

Peter shut everything down and nodded at the police technicians. "Would you guys dismantle the equipment and bring the video over when you're through?"

Peter entered David's hospital room and crossed to the side of his bed.

"I know this has been hard." Peter laid a hand on David's shoulder. "But you did great."

David cleared his throat. "I need a drink."

"All I got is water."

"That'll do."

David sipped from his cup and sighed. "We'd talked about telling my father Viktor was alive, but the lie about William Smith just came out." David shook his head. "I wasn't sure he'd buy it."

"Turns out it wasn't a lie," Nate said. "Smith is talking to us. He's hoping for a reduced sentence."

Peter moved to Zoe and took her hand. "You were amazing."

"We'll need to get statements from the two of you." Nate joined them. "But before you come to the precinct, I have a favor to ask."

THE DOORBELL RANG at Sarah's house. Madison looked at Rafe. "Should I answer?"

"Help me up. I'll go with you."

They made their way to the door. Rafe braced his back against the wall next to the door, his gun drawn.

"Who is it?"

"It's me," Peter said. "And Zoe."

Rafe holstered his gun.

"What are you two doing here?" Madison threw open the door. "Nate called and said it went just like you planned. I thought you'd be at the precinct—"

Oscar bolted in and ran tight circles around her, his tail beating against her legs.

Madison dropped to her knees and grabbed him around the neck. "I can't believe it." She grinned at her friends. "Thank you."

Oscar squirmed from her grasp and zoomed around the house.

"He hasn't done the zoomies since he was a puppy." Madison laughed.

The big dog collapsed next to her, mouth open in a smile.

Joy filled her soul as Madison stroked her dog's silky black hair.

Oscar was home.

"Nate asked us to bring Oscar to you before coming to the precinct." Peter looked at Rafe. "Need help back to your chair before we leave?"

"Yeah." Rafe took Peter's arm. "You did good, Peter."

"WE DID GOOD." Peter held Rafe's arm and eased him into his chair. "Thanks, brother."

"I meant what I said about a job. Give it serious thought."

Peter glanced at Zoe. "Rafe, I haven't said anything to Zoe, but when the Afghanistan fraud comes to light, I may have to face charges."

"What do you mean?"

"For originally taking the money and keeping quiet." The thought of leaving Zoe landed like a lead weight on his chest. But if that's what needed to happen to finally put this whole thing to rest, then so be it. Forgiveness of his actions didn't mean escape from responsibility for his choices.

"You caught the man behind it."

"I'm not sure what I've done is enough—or if it should be." Peter gazed at his friend. "I am sure of one thing. It's an honor to know you, Rafe O'Connell."

"Same here, my friend," Rafe said. "And tell Zoe."

"Yes, sir."

Peter walked down the hall to where Zoe sat by Madison and Oscar. "Hate to take a girl away from time with friends, but we need to go."

"See you later, guys." Zoe rose from the floor in a fluid motion and brushed off the seat of her pants.

As they pulled from the driveway, Peter caught her staring at him.

"Are you going to tell me what's going on?" she said.

"You don't miss a thing." Peter gave a mirthless laugh. "There's a chance once this Afghanistan fraud goes to court that I could be held accountable for not coming forward and for keeping the money."

He cut his eyes to her. She stared straight ahead. What was she thinking?

"Say something."

"So, you're telling me you could do some jail time," Zoe said.

"Possibly."

"Then I guess it's prayer time." She swiveled in her seat. "And whatever happens, it will not change how I feel about you. We're in this together. Forever if you'll have me."

"Hey." Peter grinned. "I wanted to be the one to ask."

"You are way too slow." Zoe held up her hands. "But if you must. Go ahead. I'm listening."

"Zoe Poole, will you ..." Peter coughed. "Will you ..."

"See. I knew it. You can't—"

"Marry me." Peter laughed. "Got ya."

"My answer is yes, Peter Grace." Zoe chuckled. "Even if you go to jail."

The weight lifted off his chest.

One month later

"DID YOU HEAR THE GOOD NEWS?" Zoe danced into Madison's kitchen. "Peter's lawyers in D.C. negotiated a deal using his information about the original fraud, the evidence Merton left for him, and his actions leading to the arrest of Senator Underwood." She gave Madison a quick hug. "He's free of any charges." She twirled. "He's coming home."

"Good," Rafe said. "Maybe we can finally get some work done around here. You'd think the man had been gone a year instead of a month."

"Boss, you don't fool us." Zoe wagged a finger at him. "You're just as happy as I am."

Rafe glared at her. "But I don't have to dance around like a crazed woman to show it."

"A smile would be nice," Madison said. "Us crazed women won't let anyone know your secret."

"What secret?" Rafe said.

"You have a soft center under your tough exterior." Madison smirked at him.

Rafe stared at his placemat. When he raised his head, his face had transformed. "I don't know what I would do without you two in my life." He rubbed his eye. "You are the sisters I never had. But if I had, I'd want them to be just like you." He threw them a brief but genuine smile. "Now. Back to work."

A tear slipped over the lid of Zoe's eye and ran down her cheek. She'd found her family. *Thank You, Jesus.*

52

One Year Later

Madison couldn't stop smiling. Which was fine since she was Zoe's matron of honor. After giving birth, she'd worked to regain her shape and fit into the rich blue dress Zoe picked out for the bridesmaids. The wedding had begun and now she stood in front of the church.

Madison looked at Zoe's mother in the first pew. It was one of her good days. She beamed from ear to ear. Sarah sat next to her cuddling baby Denise with Ed on the end holding baby Victor. Twins. A surprise—and a blessing.

On the other side of the aisle, Peter's grandmother and aunt couldn't take their eyes off their boy as he stood waiting for his bride.

Time for the "flower girl"—only this time it was a flower dog. Oscar trotted down the aisle with a basket of flowers around his neck. He headed straight for Madison as they'd planned—until he spotted Peter.

Tail wagging, he galloped toward his buddy, flower basket swinging to and fro. Laughter bubbled through the crowd as

Peter bent to relieve Oscar of his burden. A friend took Oscar outside, and the crowd hushed for the main event. The bride.

Tears stung Madison's eyes as Zoe appeared on Rafe's arm. An elegant sheath dress with long sleeves. Sable hair flowed down her back with the sides pulled back in an intricate chignon. She wore the pearl earrings Madison had loaned her. And those remarkable violet eyes.

Rafe in a gray tuxedo with a blue tie was doing double duty today as best man and as Zoe's escort down the aisle. He took both rolls very seriously. His ramrod posture was a perfect complement to the bride. Madison glanced to her left at her husband, Nate. So handsome in his tuxedo as one of the groomsmen. Two years ago, they stood in the front of this church pledging their love to each other.

So much had happened. Would their lives always be this full of excitement and danger? Only God knew. Whatever came, they would face it together.

***

"And now I have the privilege of presenting to you for the first time, Mr. and Mrs. Peter Grace," the minister said. "God's blessings on you and everyone present."

The music swelled as Peter escorted his bride up the aisle toward the back of the church. Madison slipped her hand under Rafe's arm, and they followed the bride and groom. At the back of the church, she turned to watch for Nate.

"Did I tell you I'm rebuilding the rental?" Rafe said in Madison's ear.

"Yes, I think you did." Madison had a hard time concentrating on what Rafe was saying as she spied her handsome husband. He looked so good in his tux. And there were Sarah and Ed with her precious babies.

"I'm renting it to a woman working undercover for Homeland Security," Rafe said.

"That's—" Madison spun around to face Rafe. "Did you say undercover?"

Rafe grinned.

The End

273

ABOUT THE AUTHOR

When Debbie Sprinkle retired from teaching in 2004, she had a plan for keeping busy. Attend the women's Bible study at her church, join a local book club, and write a mystery novel. She began going to Bible study on Wednesday mornings, and when her local library started a book club, she was one of the charter members.

One thing led to another—as they usually do—and pretty soon she was a Bible study leader and facilitating the book club. (She says it's because she has the biggest mouth!)

In 2009, she was asked to attend the She Speaks Christian Writers' Conference put on by Proverbs 31 Ministry, where she met Kendra Armstrong. It was their friendship that led to her first book written in collaboration with Kendra, *Common Sense and an Uncommon God*, published in 2012 by Lighthouse of the Carolinas. The second edition was later released under the title of *Exploring the Faith of America's Presidents*.

After attending lots of conferences, taking many classes, and sitting at the feet of a plethora of experienced writers, Debbie wrote her first novel. And, in 2019, her dream came true when *Deadly Guardian* made its debut. Two more novels rounded out the Trouble in Pleasant Valley series, and Debbie is now working on a new set of romantic suspense novels set in a small town in Missouri.

Originally from St. Louis, Debbie received her bachelor degree in chemistry from the University of Missouri-St. Louis. She worked as a research chemist for many years at both St. Louis University Medical School and Washington University Medical School. In 1991, she and her family moved to Memphis, where Debbie taught chemistry for ten years at a private girls' school before retiring.

Death of an Imposter

Trouble in Pleasant Valley

Book Two

Her first week on the job and rookie detective Bernadette Santos has been given the murder of a prominent citizen to solve. But when her victim turns out to be an imposter, her straight forward case takes a nasty turn. One that involves the attractive Dr. Daniel O'Leary, a visitor to Pleasant Valley and a man harboring secrets.

When Dr. O'Leary becomes a target of violence himself, Detective Santos has two mysteries to unravel. Are they related? And how far can she trust the good doctor? Her heart tugs her one way while her mind pulls her another. She must discover the solutions before it's too late!

Deadly Guardian

Trouble in Pleasant Valley

Book One

Madison Long, a high school chemistry teacher, looks forward to a relaxing summer break. Instead, she suffers through a nightmare of threats, terror, and death. When she finds a man murdered she once dated, Detective Nate Zuberi is assigned to the case, and in the midst of chaos, attraction blossoms into love.

Together, she and Nate search for her deadly guardian before he decides the only way to truly save her from what he considers a hurtful relationship is to kill her—and her policeman boyfriend as well.

COMING SOON FROM DEBORAH SPRINKLE

Coming in May 2022—A romantic suspense novella collection titled *Shark's Tooth Island*, which will include Deborah Sprinkle's new novella, *After the Storm*.

Coming in August 2022—*The Case of the Innocent Husband*—book one of Deborah's new series, Mac and Sam, Private Eyes.

When Bexley finds herself in trouble once more, can Evan and his team arrive in time?

Fighting the clock and their pride, Evan and Bexley must decide which is more important—their egos or their future.

Cruise to Death

Sara L. Jameson

Winner of the 2020 Scrivenings Press

Get Pubbed Contest!

When opera singer Riley Williams agrees to sub as a musical-theater performer on a luxury Rhine/Moselle River boat cruise, she gets more than she bargained for. Not only does she have to come up with 250 Broadway songs, she must dance with the male passengers. Dance—the subject she nearly failed in her conservatory courses, and the cause of her recent flop in an opera house. To make matters worse, she overhears two terrorists at a café in Antwerp, Belgium, discussing the transfer of deadly Agent X to the highest bioterrorist bidders.

Interpol Agent Jacob Coulter, an anti-terrorism desk analyst in Brussels, Belgium, insists on serving as an undercover agent after his best friend Noel is murdered by terrorists from the cell he infiltrated in Brussels. Shortly before Noel dies, he manages to tell Jacob snippets of the terrorists' plans. Plans that seem to involve the same river boat cruise Riley is on.

When Interpol learns of Riley's encounter with terrorists at the café, Jacob's supervisor insists he work with her to identify the terrorists and retrieve Agent X. But their relationship is fraught with distrust because of Riley's suspicious past and a romantic attraction neither of them wants.

www.ingramcontent.com/pod-product-compliance
Lightning Source LLC
Chambersburg PA
CBHW070626100726
47907CB00007B/1871